For the tinderbox girls, when the time comes.
And for Sarah Davies, with thanks.

The author wishes to thank the Scottish Arts Council for their support in the writing of this novel.

JULIE BERTAGNA

the opposite of chocolate

YOUNG PICADOR

The song alluded to in the book is 'Drops of Jupiter'
by Train (Columbia).
The poem quoted from is 'Burn Me' by Hugh Ouston. The author and the publisher have made every effort to trace the copyright holder of this poem, and will be pleased to make the necessary arrangement at the first opportunity.

First published 2003 by Young Picador
a division of Pan Macmillan Limited
Pan Macmillan, 20 New Wharf Road, London N1 9RR
Basingstoke and Oxford
www.panmacmillan.co.uk

Associated companies throughout the world

ISBN 0 330 41345 7

9 8 7 6 5 4 3 2 1

A CIP catalogue record for this book is available from the British Library.

Typeset by Intype Libra Ltd London
Printed and bound in Great Britain by Mackays of Chatham plc, Kent

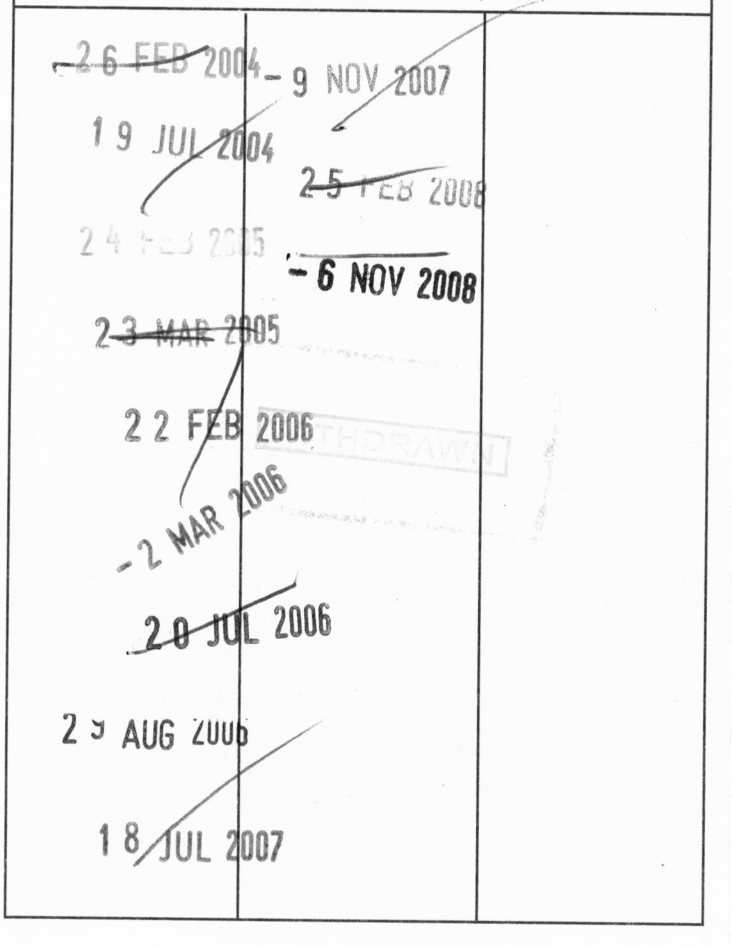

00 654727 01

the opposite of chocolate

Also by Julie Bertagna

EXODUS

SOUNDTRACK

THE SPARK GAP

‘Dream as if you’ll live forever, live as if you’ll die today.’

James Dean

It was a weird, tinderbox summer even before the fires began.

The sultry days were full of static and by evening the whole city was edgy with it. Out on the dusky margins of the suburbs, they felt the tremor in the air.

Here, in a place called Hungry, the young roamed empty streets like vampires and fed on the vibrations of the city beyond. At sundown, they'd gather on Hungry Hill. They'd look beyond their dead suburban streets and watch the clutter of the city turn to living diamonds. And they'd ache – for something, for anything, to happen.

When the fires started, it was a relief.

That summer the sun was a mighty furnace, with a blast so fierce it loosened the edges of things. By noon, the whole of Hungry looked trembly. Trees and houses shimmered, as if only just holding themselves together in the heat.

In May, everyone had welcomed the unusually good weather. Now, months later, they were withering in the drought. The days were so long, hot and barren nobody could bear them. People sheltered indoors to battle the sun. Electric fans and iced drinks were the first line of defence. Cool, illicit showers were sneaked, the rules of water rationing cast aside in the relief of a downpour on overheated skin.

In Hungry, no one had ever known a summer like it. They were used to big, wet summer winds that blew in from the Atlantic – which on a clear day could be glimpsed as a thread of silver fire on the western horizon.

The young colonized the heatstricken streets. All day long they'd wander the drives and avenues and dead-end crescents, catching shade where they could, filling the suburb with their noise, blasting music, knowing they had to make the most of summer, however hot it was. All too soon the days would close up on them like a lidded box, freedom replaced by school, homework, exams.

Evenings, as the sun began to drop and the heat of the day cooled into dusk, the young people would climb the hill that sat at the heart of Hungry, to lie in the bristly, sun-coarsened grass. Here, they would wait and watch.

Nobody knew who the firebug was. Up on Hungry Hill, the young watchers didn't care; not at first. All that mattered, in the beginning, was that somewhere among the villas and bungalows that radiated around the hill in calm, circular streets, a fire would erupt at sundown.

The dusk fires had started just after the blistering heat-wave struck. The first fires were erratic, uncertain things, as if the firebug was unsure of his powers. Now they made the dusk their own.

Each evening as the sun hit the rooftops, there came a scent of firesmoke, like incense on the air. As the watchers scanned the streets from their vantage point on the hill, the first wisp of smoke would appear, followed by flames – as shocking as a splash of blood in the quiet, tidy streets.

Now all at once the night would snap alive and the

watchers would be gripped by an excitement that made them feel, for once, as if they really were part of the world.

But the firebug was only part of the weirdness of that tinderbox summer.

Something else was born in the insufferable heat; something that should never have happened, not in a place like Hungry and not to a girl like Sapphire Dean.

But it did.

Sapphire made it just in time. The last, hot slivers of sun ran like molten lava over the rooftops of Hungry. But Sapphire didn't see. She hoisted herself up on to the wall that split the hill in two and sat there, trying to be calm.

Come on, she urged herself.

A spidery feeling crawled the floor of her stomach.

At last she dropped down, landing softly on the field on the other side of the wall. Keeping low, she moved across the grass, peering through the dusk, seeking out the special one among the dark shapes of the watchers gathered on Hungry Hill.

Down in the streets, the dusk fire was already blazing. Sirens wailed and a small fleet of fire engines blared along the Great Western Road. Now they rushed round the curve of Hungry's streets. Sapphire crouched in the grass to watch their red dash.

Tonight, they were quicker than ever. Too quick. The first fire crew reached the blazing litter bin as flames began to finger the dry leaves of an overhanging tree. A squad of firefighters surrounded the blaze. In minutes they'd have it killed and the evening's entertainment would be done.

The adults were all on full alert, that was the problem. The moment dusk fell, several police cars began to cruise the quiet streets. Residents hovered on doorsteps, watching over gardens, or leaned out of windows to sniff for the faintest whiff of smoke on the air. There was talk of an evening curfew, but most of that came from those who had no teenagers to be grounded within their walls. An evening curfew would mean houses full of sullen, stomping furies; the constant throb of music; ever-empty fridges; and the colonization of all electrical goods – TVs, computers, sound systems and phones – every evening, until the firebug was caught. The very thought of it was too horrible for most families to contemplate. Especially in such heat.

Sapphire found the one she was looking for and slipped down on the grass beside him.

'Hi.'

'Oh, hi,' said Jay. He didn't look at her; he was fixed on the action in the streets below.

'Hey, stranger,' Emma called over softly. 'Haven't seen you for days. Where've you been?'

Sapphire turned and tried to smile at Emma, who was all tangled up with Grant. It was difficult, in the dusk light, to see whose arms and legs were whose. Sapphire was glad of the dimness, hoping that it hid her raw, over-bright eyes; the evidence of a day spent in tears.

But Emma seemed to see through the dusk. They'd known each other so long, from the inside out, that each could tell even over the phone when the other was out of sorts.

Emma disentangled from Grant. She stretched across the grass to touch her friend's arm.

'Sapphy, I'm sorry,' she whispered, so low that not even Jay would hear. Her face was soft with sympathy. 'I was going to come and see you. I've told him what I think of him. Sapphy, what're you going to *do*?'

Sapphire recoiled as if Emma had bitten her. How could

Emma know? No one knew, not even Jay. She'd not breathed a word to anyone, had only just found out for sure herself, though she'd been worried for weeks. Sapphire glanced down at her body. How could Emma tell? Was there already some change that gave her secret away?

All day, Sapphire had been holding on to the little stick of white plastic in the pocket of her jeans. Now she shoved it deeper into the pocket, so that there was no chance of it slipping out or being seen. She curled the little finger of her hand through the little finger of Jay's hand, beside hers on the grass, just as she always did, as if nothing was wrong; though everything was wrong, as wrong as it ever could be. And she had to tell Jay what was wrong. She had to get him alone and try to tell him, tonight.

'Wicked,' breathed Grace, from close behind, as the blaze from the litter bin zipped up the tree, outwitting the fire crew.

Excitement buzzed among the watchers on the hill. Nobody moved.

Then someone did. Someone stood up.

It was Lee, built like a tank, which made him the most likely of them all to be seen from the streets below. The other watchers hissed furious threats. When Lee then did the unforgivable and yelled out 'There!' still on his feet, the others let rip. Hands shot out to grab his ankles and he toppled under the onslaught, slamming heavily on to the ground, back into the cover of the grass.

'Do that again and you're off this hill,' said Grace. 'For good.'

Lee nodded, rubbing his crashed shoulder, but he never took his eyes off the action on the streets below.

'There!' he exclaimed again, but managing to do it quietly. 'Look at that – another one!'

Two streets back from the extinguished litter bin and the blazing tree darted another, larger fire; it stuttered to life. As they watched, it fragmented into a brilliant, jagged fury that spread the entire length of a garden fence.

Sapphire's little finger gripped Jay's as she watched. He didn't squeeze back.

'So the first one . . .' Jay murmured.

Aaron, a twig-like boy, whose calm, angel-face belied an obsessional mind, nodded. 'The first was just a decoy but this is the real one, the big one,' he agreed. 'This guy's amazing.'

'How do you know it's a guy?' said Emma.

Nobody bothered to answer.

A whisper made Sapphire glance behind her. She saw, with an unpleasant turn of her stomach, that Grace was kneeling on the grass close to Jay.

Far too close.

Her head was almost touching his. And her hand was on his shoulder.

Sapphire stared.

The hand lay on Jay's shoulder, one finger gently moving, writing slow, secret messages on the black leather jacket that he always wore, no matter how hot it was. Sapphire glanced from the hand up to the face of its owner, but Grace was fully curtained by the fall of waist-long, ink-black hair. Occasionally, with a flourish, she would sweep her hair back with a hand, which she did with the air of giving an exclusive viewing of her exquisite face.

Neither Jay nor Grace appeared to be aware of that slim hand on his shoulder. They seemed absorbed in the action in the streets below. But they knew, they knew, thought Sapphire.

Emma reached out and squeezed Sapphire's arm in

solidarity, and Sapphire realized her earlier mistake. Emma hadn't guessed her awful secret. It was *this* she'd been sorry about – Jay and Grace.

'There must be a team of them. What do you think?' said Jay, screwing up his eyes to peer deeper into the streets and gardens.

Sapphire couldn't think of an answer. Then she saw, from the slight tilt of his face, that Jay wasn't talking to her. He was talking to Grace.

'I think,' said Grace, and her hand moved a millimetre closer to Jay's neck, 'we should bring him out into the open.'

'How?' demanded Aaron.

'By showing him what *we* can do,' said Grace.

'What we can do?' muttered Jay, and he lay back sullenly on the grass. 'We do nothing, ever. It's like being under anaesthetic, living in this place.'

Sapphire felt a jolt inside. What about everything that had happened between her and Jay this summer? That was nothing? She unhooked her little finger from his but made the mistake of glancing at him lying stretched out in the grass. Then the old feeling churned inside, the snaky twist of excitement she always felt next to him, because he was gorgeous.

Now, instead of pulling away, she made herself link all her fingers through his and softly squeezed his hand. Jay turned towards her at last and smiled, an uneasy smile.

On his other side, Grace breathed a long, low sigh. Even her breathing seemed practised, executed for maximum effect. And it worked. Jay was captivated by her again.

'Let's show him *we're* here . . .' Grace murmured in the low, imperious tone she had perfected. 'Who *we* are.'

Sapphire couldn't look, didn't want to see, but she *felt*

Grace sweep a hand through her hair in that dramatic way of hers, then trail her fingers down along her body, knowing Jay's eyes would follow. Sapphire had seen her practise this move a hundred times and it always worked. But never before had she tried it on Jay. Grace's other hand still lay on his shoulder. But Jay's unresponsive one, still linked in Sapphire's, trembled.

Sapphire felt herself turn inside out.

Say something. Do something. Don't let her do this, right in front of you.

But she just sat there, and did nothing, didn't know what to do, except slip her hand out of Jay's. He didn't seem to notice.

And yet moments later he turned to her and smiled again, almost as if everything might still be all right between them. Oh, but it wasn't. Something in his face, in the way he didn't look her in the eye, was quite different.

'I'm going,' Sapphire muttered.

'Bye,' said Grace.

Jay looked down at the streets, as if his mind was elsewhere. It was, thought Sapphire. His mind was on Grace.

'Jay,' she said, and hated herself for saying it.

But something in her voice seemed to touch him at last. He leaned over and kissed her quickly, stealthily, as if he didn't want anyone to see. Or didn't want *her* to see, thought Sapphire, though Grace was taking in everything, she was sure, through her dark curtain of hair.

Sapphire took his kiss, and left.

And though everything was spoilt between them, it was so strange that she couldn't feel any difference in his kiss. Live and tingling, it stayed on her lips as she crept back across the hillside.

Something was going on between Jay and Grace. Just

an hour ago, that would have seemed impossible. The shock of it rocked her. On top of her other, earlier shock, it was too cruel.

Once again, Sapphire gripped the horrible little white stick in her pocket, gripped it so hard that her fingers hurt, but even that didn't make it feel real.

It didn't feel real, Sapphire decided, because it couldn't be.

She heaved herself up on to the high, stone wall, and sat there, quietly, amid the shadows of the trees. The wall, like the earth and the pavements, was still warm with the latent heat of the sun. It burned her bare legs. Sapphire swung them over to the other side of the wall, ready to jump down into the cooling shadow of the trees.

Maybe there was nothing really going on between Jay and Grace. Maybe it was just one of Grace's power games. And maybe the other thing wasn't true either. Maybe the stick had got it wrong. Maybe she'd got it all wrong. Sapphire looked across Hungry Hill and what she saw there made her shiver, though the night air was still thick with heat.

Two shadows had moved apart from the others. And Sapphire knew, she just knew, who they were.

It *was* true.

She wanted to look away yet she couldn't.

'Sapphy!'

Emma was racing across the hill.

When she got to the wall she swung herself up alongside Sapphire and dangled her legs over the side, barefoot. She began picking out the grass that had stuck in her bobbed, blonde hair.

'Ouch, it's hot. Sapphy, I've been trying to get hold of you for days. I phoned lots but no one could find you.'

Emma took a deep breath and wrapped her arms around Sapphire in a hard hug. 'Grace got her claws into Jay the minute you were out of the way – but it's your own fault! I cornered him last night and he says he doesn't even know if you two are together any more, you've been so glum and grumpy and you've hardly let him near you for ages. Sapphy, what's wrong?'

'So he's really with her now?'

Emma just looked. Her large blue eyes, little nose and her habit of staring at people with her mouth open, showing her two front teeth, gave her a cute, bunny-rabbit look. Now she bit her lip and screwed up her nose and eyes as if she were looking into the sun, though the sun was now gone. The sky was streaked with colour but everything else was falling into night.

'She hijacked him. But you let her – he thinks you've gone off him 'cause you've not been here for days, so she took her chance and just *pounced.*' Emma mimed a seductive pounce. 'He didn't stand a chance. But you'd get him back in a minute if you wanted to. I bet you could. She's had her eye on him all summer and she never managed to get him till you weren't there.'

'Has she?' Sapphire felt stupid. She hadn't a clue that Grace had been a rival. She'd been too engrossed in Jay.

Sapphire doubted she had the power to win him back, not against Grace. And definitely not now. The little white stick in her pocket was a small bomb waiting to explode.

'Sapphy? What's going on? Talk!'

Sapphire shook her head. Emma was her closest friend but she couldn't even tell her.

'D'you still love him?' asked Emma, her eyes large and pale in the dusk.

Love, thought Sapphire, and dug her nails into the palm of her hand.

She pushed herself off the wall and dropped down on to the other side, into the grounds of Hunger Home, where she lived.

'Alligator,' she called up to Emma, still high on the wall. She hugged her friend's leg as a sort of apology for being so strange.

'Crocodile,' sighed Emma.

They'd used the same old, silly shorthand for 'goodbye' since they were seven.

See you later, alligator. In a while, crocodile.

Emma hit the ground on the other side with a soft thud. Sapphire heard the rasp of the grass as she raced back across the hillside to retangle with Grant. Now Sapphire was alone. She wrapped her arms around the thick trunk of a chestnut tree and stared into the dark.

For Emma, summer went on. For Sapphire, it was over. Everything was over, and the future stretched in front – terrifying and blank.

There was another watcher in Hungry.

A woman, frail as a wisp.

She was not old; but neither was she young. There was something about her thin mouth and tired eyes, a delicacy in her haggard face that suggested, to anyone who might look closely enough under the rim of her straw hat, that she might have had a fragile beauty once. But anything that was left of her ruined beauty was now overshadowed by a straggle of greying hair and an indefinable expression in her eyes that tended to make anyone who did look keep their distance.

Most people didn't look, because there was an

anonymous quality about this wisp of a woman that made her as unnoticeable as a lamp-post – so she could wait and watch, almost unseen, for hours on end.

Tonight, the wisp woman watched the world from the bus shelter at the foot of Hungry Hill. She knew how to stand just as if she were waiting for a bus.

All through the evening she stood and watched. Occasionally she would murmur a poem she had once found in a newspaper – a poem that cut to the heart of all that she was.

The young ones up on the hill, the other watchers, thought they knew all that went on in their world, but up there they couldn't see what the wisp woman in the bus shelter had just seen – the one who did it.

The firebug.

A bolt of joy hit her heart as she'd watched the boy race up the street and vault the wall behind her. But now she eyed the blazing litter bin with a sinking heart and waited for the rest of the night to unfold.

Sapphire lived in a palace.

On the other side of the wall that ran like a zip up the middle of Hungry Hill sat the palatial, eighteenth-century mansion that was Hunger Home for the Elderly. It was also Sapphire's home. Majestically, it crested the suburb that had grown up around it and taken its name.

Several hundred years ago, Hunger Home was the grand residence of a sugar lord, a rich merchant who had made his fortune from importing raw cane sugar and cocoa beans from the West Indies to his riverside factory beside the city's docks. People said Hungry took its name from the small chocolate-making factory the sugar lord had set up in his mansion. Late every evening, the aroma of chocolate would bedevil the air as the lord worked on his delicious confections, deep into the night. In surrounding cottages and farms, the locals would toss and turn in restless, hungry sleep, their dreams haunted by the dark, exotic scents of the sugar lord's late-night experiments in chocolate.

Other people said that was all nonsense; the chocolate-making story was just a myth. Hungry, they said, was really named after the three-hundred-million-year-old fossil of an immense shark found in the hill when the sugar lord built his mansion. In prehistoric times, the hill had been an island of marsh surrounded by lakeland. Millions of years locked in a muddy swamp had preserved the fossil so well that the remains of the shark's last supper were still in evidence – a banquet of fish bloated the stomach of what must have been a very hungry shark.

Whatever the truth, nowadays Hungry was a well-to-do city suburb and Hunger Home was where many of its elderly residents spent their last years.

From the outside, the Home was a grand sight. At night, spotlit to stark whiteness against the black of the sky, it looked as staged and surreal as a gothic film set. By day, the gracious trees and lawns, the sweeping driveway, pillared entrance and the central tower of the mansion promised plush luxury.

Inside, that promise proved false. A Heritage Trust Fund kept Hunger Home's architecture stone-cleaned and spotlit, as befitted such a well-known landmark – it could be seen from miles around. But funds didn't stretch to the interior, which had long fallen from stately grace to something much more spartan.

Sapphire's parents were care managers of Hunger Home for the Elderly. Their family quarters were a higgledy crush of small rooms, near the top of the thick, high tower that was the centrepiece of the building. Sapphire and her two sisters, Miranda and Gretel, had grown up with a huge, wandering, extended family of old people – rooms and corridors full of them. The scale of the job meant that Jude and Boris Dean were forever harassed and exhausted. Like a couple of sea captains in charge of an antiquated but beautiful old ship that was just too vast, too unwieldy, they endeavoured as best they could to keep their ship afloat and on course.

Despite her parents' best intentions, Sapphire had decided that a lot of the old people wished they were elsewhere. They filled their days with television and books that allowed them to imagine they were living altogether other lives, in other places, other times; or they stared at the walls, reliving their own lives, re-embodying their younger selves. Those bewildered by dementia or happily befuddled by drugs would sit on the window-seats, watching the wide sky and the unchanging scenery as if they were passengers on a ship, travelling on to somewhere else.

And then there was Rose Wolfbane, who had invented an entire past of two husbands and fifteen grandchildren – she would name and describe every single one – yet none of it was real. She had never married. But it made her happy to spin herself a fairy tale of the life she had never lived, especially during these muggy, too-hot-to-sleep nights.

The midges that hung in dense, fizzling clouds all over the grounds of Hunger Home soon discovered Sapphire and began to bite. All of a sudden they were in her hair, on her face, at her eyes. The appetite of the insect cloud got her to her feet. Coiling her hair, rope-like, she tucked it under her chin. Lifting her arms free of the nettles and bramble bushes that sprouted near the wall, she stamped a path through the stings and thorns. Tiny needles tore the skin of her legs but once clear of vicious plants and insects, she stood in the shadows of the trees and looked across the great sweep of the lawns to the spot-lit tower that was her home.

Sapphire walked out of the dark into the blaze of spotlights that beamed a spectral night light upon Hunger Home. If, right now, she were to climb the stairs up to her tower bedroom and look out of the window, she would have a clear, uninterrupted view of Hungry and would see again what she had watched as she sat on the wall – a pair of dancing fireflies. Two firefly cigarettes, their burning tips darting in and out of each other's path, writing red-hot messages to each other in the dusk. His and hers. Jay and Grace. They had moved apart from the others as soon as she left.

And suddenly Sapphire was shot through with feeling, remembering in her body, right to the core, how it was with her and Jay. The two of them often came here to be alone. It was back there among the trees that it all started, exactly two weeks after her fourteenth birthday.

Sapphire smothered the feeling. She couldn't bear it, not now. She moved quickly across the lawns. The old people bedded down early at night so most of the windows were dark. All except one window in the tower, where she could see the restless shadow of her father flitting back and forth.

Sapphire hugged herself, trying to blank out the image of those dancing fireflies on the hilltop, just over the wall. She slid her fingers into her pocket and, for the hundredth time, she gripped the little white predictor stick whose tiny window had, late last night, told her future in two stark blue lines that had refused to fade all day.

She couldn't think clearly; could hardly think at all. And she had lost her chance to speak to Jay. How could she tell him now? Especially now. Where would she find the courage? She could never have imagined it all ending up like this, with Jay and Grace out there together on the hillside, while she was here alone.

Alone and pregnant.

She could take the predictor stick out of her pocket right now, snap it in two, crunch it to bits with her heel until it was hidden deep in the gravel of the path. And that would be it obliterated, gone.

Except it wouldn't be, not really. Because the real evidence was growing inside her right now, second by second, cell by cell.

A *thing* that was the start of a baby, a human being, as small as a slug, was alive deep within her. Another person was growing inside her person. Such a weird idea.

Horrible.

A thrill of dread ran through her. Sapphire shuddered and pressed the palm of her hand to her stomach, but it felt flat and calm, just the same as it ever did.

Impossible.

A cry broke from one of Hunger Home's dark windows. It lunged out into the night then lost itself in useless echoes somewhere among the trees. That started off another voice, then another, in a chain reaction that spread round the bedrooms. Sapphire was used to the night calls of the old folk. Some nights, and you could never predict why, they'd wail and sing and rage. Tonight, the noise made Sapphire's skin crawl.

Standing in a blast of spotlight, she waited for her dad to work his magic and settle them, probably with the help of some pills. And it would be Dad, not Mum. She would be tucked away in her cupboard-den by now.

The crunch of a twig made her turn. The crunch came from the trees, and the fact that it didn't make her jump told Sapphire that she must have been waiting and hoping for that very sound – the sound of Jay's footfall behind her.

Maybe the cigarette fireflies weren't his and Grace's. Or perhaps there was nothing serious between them. Maybe Grace was just playing her flirting games and he was playing along because it boosted his ego. Or to make her, Sapphire, jealous.

Because what Emma said was true. She had kept her distance from Jay for a couple of weeks now; ever since that awful moment, right in the middle of Sunday lunch. Miranda was putting Dad right off his roast lamb with her rant that men had it easy because they didn't have to suffer years and years of stupid, cramping periods. It was at that very moment, while Mum was fielding a barrage of awkward questions on the subject from Gretel, that Sapphire had realized her own period was weeks overdue . . .

Now Sapphire stepped out of the glare of the spotlight and stared into the dark, but she couldn't see a thing, her eyes were still too dazzled by the lights.

'Hi,' she whispered. 'Are you there?'

Silence.

'Can't see you.'

Still no answer. Just the sound of hard breathing, as if he'd been running. He'd left Grace and he'd run to her.

'Where are you then?'

A rustling, movement – and suddenly she could make out the dark shape of him under a tree. Sapphire slipped closer to the shadows of the trees. She took a deep breath and the words came in a rush before she'd worked out what to say.

'I have to talk to you. It's just – I couldn't. I mean, it was only yesterday I really knew for sure . . . and things've been so . . .' Her voice faltered.

Calm down, Sapphire told herself, but her heart boomed. The sound filled her head. If only he would help her out and say something, come out of the trees, come closer. His silence made him feel so distant and strange.

Start again. Tell him.

'I don't know what to say. I thought – well, I thought maybe you wouldn't want to know me. That's why I never said anything before.'

It felt like an awful lot of words. A lot of jumbled-up words to say one very simple thing:

I'm pregnant.

Say it.

'I'm pregnant,' she whispered.

Blood thumped in her head.

And he said nothing. Didn't move. The shock had turned him to stone.

Sapphire stepped deeper into the shadow of the trees. She couldn't stand the distance between them any more. His silence, his utter stillness, unnerved her.

What was he thinking? Was he angry? Too shocked to speak? She hardly dared look at him. Her vision was still dazzled by the spotlights so it was hard to see, but she had to look at him, to gain some clue of what he was feeling.

When at last her eyes cleared of the dazzle, Sapphire peered into the trees.

And lost a heartbeat.

The boy in the shadows was not Jay.

The face that stared back through the dark, utterly still and full of wonder, was that of a stranger.

Sapphire turned and raced back through the spotlights, across the lawns. She crunched up the gravel path to the stone porch, punched her code into the security door, crashed through and raced up the grand stairway, up and up until she reached her bedroom right at the top of the tower.

The stranger in the grounds stood under the trees, staring up at the spot-lit mansion where the girl had vanished, watching all its windows until he saw one of them, high in the central tower, fill with light. And he knew that it was hers.

Sapphire switched off her lamp and lay on her bed in the dark, listening to the soft, grunty breathing of her small sister. Gretel was so sound asleep that she hadn't stirred when Sapphire had burst in and flung herself down on the bed, hot, dry-eyed, with a miserable cry. The lamplight didn't wake her either, so the creak of a window surely wouldn't. Sapphire stood on her bed to reach up and unlock the tower window's safety catch. She hauled open the heavy sash as smoothly as she could to minimize its elderly groans, until there was just enough of a gap to squeeze through, out on to the thin ledge of balcony below.

Now came the tricky bit.

To reach the top of the tower she had to climb the drainpipe that ran up the side of her bedroom window to the roof of the tower itself. There was always a precarious moment when the drainpipe made the kind of noise that warned it might break from its rusty supports and catapult her backwards, to land with a crash on the gravel a long way down below.

But it never had, as yet. So Sapphire gripped the drain-pipe between her hands and knees, ignored the ominous creaks and groans, and climbed up. She hauled herself over the parapet of Hunger Home's tower, on to its flat roof. With her forearm, she wiped a film of sweat from her face and peeled her T-shirt from her body to waft some air on to her clammy skin.

Starlight throbbed overhead, blurred by the haze that thickened the night air. Below, orange lozenges of street-lamps studded the dark with the radiating patterns of the streets. The haze made them look as if they were melting. Beyond the lights of Hungry, the path of the Great Western Road was traced in a long, straight channel of lights to the vast sparkle of the city. And beyond that was the glittering 'S' of the motorway that led south, to the cities beyond the border.

She had always looked at that 'S' with a corresponding twist of excitement that she couldn't explain, though she knew it was something to do with her future. Now, all thought of the future churned her stomach with a snaky terror.

There was no sign of the boy she'd mistaken for Jay. The stranger she had, unwittingly, told her deepest secret; the thing that no one else knew in the whole world. But he could still be there, somewhere deep in the trees or in the darkness of the lawns.

There was no sign either of the two dancing fireflies on the hill. But Jay and Grace would be lying there, entwined in the dark.

Once again, Sapphire felt an overwhelming urge to chuck the predictor stick from her pocket and grind it to dust underfoot – as if that would solve anything. She felt about in her pocket for it. It wasn't there. She tried the other pocket. Empty. Where was it?

She'd had it in the grounds. Did she still have it in the bedroom? Sapphire leaned over the parapet and looked down on to the gravel path and the grounds. She must have dropped it somewhere out there when she'd rushed indoors or when she climbed the drainpipe. Well, she'd better find it, fast, before someone else did.

Because she'd be first suspect.

Who else in Hunger Home would be the likely owner of a stray pregnancy test?

Surely not Mum, and definitely not seven-year-old Gretel or any of the Home's old women. Miranda, her older sister, stayed in a friend's flat near the city's university during the week, so there would only be one possible suspect.

Sapphire swung over the parapet and slipped down the drainpipe, back into her bedroom. Gretel sat up in bed for a moment, scratched her head frantically, then flopped down and went straight back to sleep. Sapphire bolted along the hall, downstairs, down and down the curving sweep of the staircase until she was within one leap of the main hallway, where old Rose Wolfbane was bent over, as if she was examining the black-and-white patterns of the mosaic floor. It was only when Rose straightened up and popped a little white stick in her mouth that Sapphire saw what had happened.

The old woman had found the predictor stick and was walking along the corridor with it stuck like a thermometer in the side of her mouth.

Now Sapphire knew why films showed horror scenes in slow motion. It was because it really did feel like that.

She ran after Rose Wolfbane as the old woman shuffled barefoot down the hall in her billowing, poppy-red nightie. But stuck in her moment of slow-motion horror, Sapphire couldn't run fast enough. She felt she was running through thickening glue. She was never going to make it in time.

And she didn't.

Boris, her father, appeared from the doorway with Mrs Merry, another of the old women, on his arm. He smiled then frowned at old Rose. Sapphire was just a leap away, close enough to hear the soft, sticky pop as he pulled the white predictor stick out from the old woman's toothless gums.

'What are you doing up so late, Rosie?' said Dad, yawning but affectionate. 'Got a temperature?'

He glanced at the thing in his hand and his brow creased as he saw exactly what it was.

Then he saw Sapphire. And as he absorbed the unmistakable look on her face, and she watched understanding flood his, the world seemed to stop.

Every evening Sapphire's mother, Jude, would disappear into a walk-in cupboard in the middle of Hunger Home's tower and close the door with a thankful sigh.

Inside the tiny cupboard-den Jude had made for herself, she would sip a gin and tonic – or throw it back, depending on the kind of day it had been – and bask in the soothing red light of her photo-developing lamp, alone for the first time in a long day of caring for young and old; caring for everybody except herself. Her back would ache from hauling frail old bodies out of beds, into baths and wheelchairs and armchairs, then back into beds again.

Now that everyone was settled for the night (or should be), Jude at last had time for herself in her photo-den.

Boris or the nightshift nurses could see to anything that wasn't an emergency.

Now, as the gin seeped through her in a swift, relaxing wave, Jude studied the thick cluster of photos on her make-shift photo hanger (a wooden spaghetti-dryer) and sighed. Portraits of the old people and her daughters. Lots of Gretel. Lots of trees and leaves. A mosaic of moss, a zoom lens close-up of gravel patterns on the driveway, wide-angle views of Hungry at sunrise and moonrise from the top of the tower. Photos of every kind, of everything that was in range of Hunger Home and its grounds. But nothing beyond.

Well, there was never time to go out.

'Jude.'

'What?'

Impossible to keep the irritation out of her voice. Could he not manage for a single hour without her?

'I need to speak to you.' Boris pulled at the door handle but she'd bolted the cupboard door from the inside. 'Jude!'

Jude sighed and slid back the bolt.

'We have a problem,' said her husband, as she knew he would.

Sapphire stood outside the cupboard, still feeling that her feet were stuck in glue. She was fixed to the spot where her father had told her to say put, though she wanted to run. The murmur of Dad's voice came from inside her mother's den. All Sapphire could hear from Mum was silence.

'Sapphire,' she said at last.

And that was all. No explosion of anger, nothing for what felt like a very long time.

When Boris reappeared, he was grim and pale. But his disbelief had turned to something Sapphire had never seen in his quiet face before.

For the first time in her life, Sapphire was scared of her father. He looked ready to punch a hole through the door. But he didn't, just held the door of the cupboard open until the only thing she could do to escape that frightening look was to go into the cupboard and face her mother.

Jude sat staring at the photographs on the spaghetti-dryer. She didn't say anything at all, just stared at the photos as if they'd come out all wrong.

The silence became unbearable.

'You're fourteen years old,' Jude whispered at last. She picked up her glass and swallowed the rest of her gin all in one.

Now that her mother had spoken, Sapphire let out a shuddering breath and shoved the palms of her hands over her eyes as she'd done when she was little, to hide a sudden rush of tears. But her mouth wobbled and a babyish-sounding cry came out. Maybe it was that sudden mirror of her childhood self that got to her mother because all of a sudden she pulled Sapphire down on to her knee, just as if she was six, and hugged her. Sapphire felt her mother's tears on her neck.

The cupboard door opened. Boris stared for a moment then backed out and shut the door, not saying a word.

After a while they scrubbed their eyes. Then Jude picked up the white, pencil-like thing, the slim grenade that Boris had handed to her. She had been puzzled at first, wondering if it was a new piece of medical equipment that Boris had brought in to show her.

'Sapphire,' Boris had said at last.

'Sapphire?' she'd said, not understanding.

And then had seen exactly what the thing was.

'Sapphire,' Boris insisted.

Jude went blank. Couldn't think or speak. Could only stare at the impossible thing.

'Found it sticking out of Rose Wolfbane's mouth. But it's Sapphire's all right,' Boris had said. 'It was written all over her face.'

Jude hadn't even tried to find out how a predictor stick belonging to her daughter came to be stuck in the old woman's mouth. Things like that happened almost every day in Hunger Home.

Well, not quite like this. Jude Dean had found herself handling all kinds of life-and-death situations in the years she had co-managed the Home with Boris, but none of that could help her deal with this – the shocking evidence of the little white stick that she held in her hand. Two tiny, rigid, sky-blue lines in its miniature window seemed to symbolize the bars of the prison, thought Jude, that her fourteen-year-old daughter had made of her own life.

And I should know, thought Jude.

'Sapphy, you're breaking my knees,' she murmured.

Sapphire slipped off.

'Mum, what'll I do?' she burst out, and the voice that came out was hardly her own, it was such a trembly, childish thing.

Jude pulled out the scrunchy she used to keep her hair out of her face. She rubbed her head at the tender part where the ponytail had been all day until her hair was tousled. Suddenly she looked younger and very like Sapphire's older sister, Miranda.

'You stupid, stupid – you're just a little *girl*!'

'I'm sorry, I'm sorry,' Sapphire whispered.

Jude looked at her daughter. Without the camouflage of

make-up that Sapphire had begun wearing (no harm in that, Jude had thought, it's what teenage girls do) she saw that Sapphire's blue eyes were dark-shadowed and frightened. Her face was pale and wan. Why had she not noticed before?

Because I'm run off my feet, Jude told herself. I don't have time to notice things, not even the signs of my own child in trouble.

She stood up and pushed open the door of her den. A thought struck.

'How many months' pregnant are you? Do you know?'

Sapphire looked blank.

'How long have you been seeing this boy?'

'Since May,' said Sapphire.

Jude did a quick calculation. 'Well, that's something. There's still enough time to—' She stopped. 'I'm going out for a walk,' she told Boris, who was hanging about in the hallway. 'I need to think.'

'What about the boy?' said Boris. 'Who is he?'

'Never mind that now,' said Jude. 'There are more urgent things than that.'

'I want to know,' said Boris. 'I want a name. Will you find out or will I?'

'Leave it with me,' muttered Jude, as she ran down the stairs.

At the foot of the stairs she stumbled, dizzy from the gin she'd flung back. Outside Hunger Home's thick stone walls, the night was heavy and hot. Jude walked through the spotlights on the lawns and entered the darkness of the grounds where the trees gave some relief from the heat.

Oh, Sapphire, she thought, you stupid girl.

No more stupid than her mother.

Jude had always thought they'd get out of Hungry. It

was only meant to be a temporary stop – a secure job and a home while Miranda and Sapphire were little. The schools were good and the streets were safe. It was never meant to be the end of the story.

Jude had planned to restart her photography career, doing freelance shoots for magazines, once Sapphire was at school. But she had fallen pregnant with Gretel. And her career, her beloved photography, had once again fizzled out. There was just no time for it.

If Sapphire had this child, Jude knew she would never have her career back. Her photography would stay in its cupboard.

Sapphire would have to go back to school and she would have to raise the child. You couldn't have a fourteen-year-old bringing up a baby – a child bringing up a child. The responsibility would fall on her, as grandmother.

I'll be a *grandmother*, Jude realized, appalled at the thought.

It would set her back another five years at least. She'd be heading for fifty by the time the child was at school. And by then her own parents who, just recently, had begun to seem frail, would be reaching old age and might well need her care.

Jude sat down on the grass. Was her whole life always to be burdened by caring for others? What about *her* dreams?

She looked into the darkness and saw her future contract, shrunk to the limits of Hungry.

Gilbert Lemon waited, with a stillness so intense it seemed to belong to the night. He saw someone rush out of Hunger Home then walk through the spotlights, out on to the dark lawns. She sat down, close to where he was in the trees. He didn't move. He just watched.

It wasn't the girl. Gilbert sat with his back to a tree until the woman returned to the house. He waited until midnight, when the spotlights switched off and everything plunged into darkness.

Only then did he move. He came out from the trees and padded down the lawns, avoiding the noisy gravel path, until he reached the iron gate in the stone wall that enclosed the grounds. He gave Hunger Home one last glance, seeking out the now-dark window that he knew was the girl's. Then he listened, nerves at full stretch, for the sound he had trained himself to pick up – the crawl of a police car.

But the road was clear. So he scrambled, lithe as a leopard, over the locked gate and dropped down on to the pavement.

He would have waited all night, if he thought there was any chance the girl would come back. But she wouldn't. People never came back, no matter what they said. That much he knew.

But he could wish and he could wait. That he could do.

Sapphire sat cloistered in the cosy red light of her mother's photo-den. She felt safer, more protected in here than in the bare electric light of the rooms outside. Everything had happened so fast she hadn't had time to think. It was impossible to think. Instead, Sapphire gently spun the spaghetti-dryer and the photos fluttered, fanning her hot face with a tiny breeze.

On a shelf above the desk sat a bottle of gin. Mostly, it turned the world into a mellower place for Mum, but sometimes it hardened something in her. Sometimes, after one too many glasses, came what Sapphire and Miranda called the gin-flick: Jude would turn brittle and bitter and occasionally furious with the whole world.

The glass of the bottle was as blue as a twilight sky, Sapphire knew, but the red lamplight had turned it a murky purple. 'Sapphire Gin', read the label. Not for the first time Sapphire wondered indignantly why she had ended up with the name of her mother's favourite tipple. Had she been conceived in a blue haze of gin?

Don't be silly, Jude had protested, when Sapphire threw that in her face during an argument. I gave you the name to match your eyes.

Eyes as blue as a bottle of gin, thought Sapphire wryly.

As her gaze dropped from the bottle, Sapphire caught the eye of the beautiful woman in a photo that hung on the wall of the den. It was as familiar as a family photo. Mum had taken it years ago as a student in Paris, in a strange and distant life, the one she'd had before her real life (as Sapphire thought of it), before she married Dad. Jude rarely talked about that lost life of hers, and when she did it was in such a wistful voice that Sapphire was glad she hardly ever did.

Even the sky was different in Paris, she'd say, even the sky.

That Parisian adventure was so removed from Jude's life now that, if it hadn't been for the evidence of her photographs, Sapphire would have found it impossible to believe. She couldn't imagine either of her parents as carefree and young.

Mum had titled the photo *The Boulevard of Dreams* (though later she had scrawled the word *broken* in angry-looking biro pen above the *Dreams*). The woman was Jeanne Moreau, a French actress. It was Jude's treasured possession – the one thing, apart from her family, that she would save from a fire.

It was her masterpiece, a once-in-a-lifetime shot. The kind of shot that could make a career. It was a fluke, a miracle, a million-to-one lucky chance: a snatched close-up of the enigmatic Jeanne Moreau sitting at a pavement cafe table, her collar turned up against the chill of a Parisian spring. A soft haze of cigarette smoke hung around her head, and her lips were parted at the rim of a tiny cup of espresso coffee.

It wasn't the beauty or sophistication of the woman that struck. She looked slightly too real to be a film star; there was a rough edge to her allure. And she wasn't young. The lines around her eyes and mouth were clear even through the cigarette haze.

What had always fascinated Sapphire, even before she was old enough to figure it out, was that Jeanne Moreau was utterly alive in the moment, sitting at that cafe table on a Parisian boulevard. The world around was a blur of motion. But she sat there, an oasis of stillness, and she looked engrossed in her own life in a way that made Sapphire's skin tingle.

She looked part of the city and the city looked part of her.

And Mum had made Jeanne Moreau part of the family. Moreaus – enigmatic quotes from the actress that Mum had collected from magazine interviews – were scattered all through the apartment, pinned to more snatched photos, from that day on Jude's Boulevard of Dreams.

Life is risking, Jeanne Moreau would urge in the hallway, her sultry eyes gazing out over a jumbled pile of shoes and umbrellas. Most days of her life, ever since she could read, Sapphire had pulled on her shoes and run down Hunger Home's great curving staircase and out of the front door with those words echoing in her head, in the deep, smoky, French accent that she'd imagined for Jeanne Moreau.

Nostalgia is when you want things to stay the same, another Moreau would murmur from the fridge door, as Sapphire scoffed cold pasta bake straight from the fridge last thing at night. *People who stay the same are dead before they die.*

Through mists of steam, as Sapphire lay in the bath, a Moreau would instruct her from the back of the door that, *The life you had is nothing. It is the life you have that is important.*

In the evenings, when Jude disappeared into her den, you took your life in your hands if you disregarded the Moreau that she stuck outside the door, declaring, *I need, absolutely, to be alone.*

And here within Mum's photo-den was the most tantalizing Moreau of all, pinned above the cigarette haze in Jude's once-in-a-lifetime shot.

It is a fragrance; it doesn't last. Non. Because it fades quickly. It's like a cloud; it has one shape and then seconds after it is gone. After it is gone . . .

After *what's* gone? Sapphire always wondered. What's *it*? What was Jeanne Moreau talking about? It didn't matter, said Jude. It's whatever you want it to mean. Anything you like. Anything you need it to mean.

But even if she ever did work out what *it* was, what then? *After it is gone . . .* then what happened?

White light shot through the lamp's soft, red gloom. Sapphire turned round. Her mother stood in the open doorway of the den.

'You're not going to have a baby,' Jude announced. 'Your life hasn't even started. It'll be ruined. You won't be able to make anything of yourself. The whole – whole *scope* of your life will be lost, maybe forever . . .'

Jude stared at the spaghetti-dryer.

'But the test said I was definitely preg—' Sapphire began, then understood what her mother was saying. She was pregnant but she wasn't going to have the baby.

Sapphire swallowed back sudden tears of relief. She didn't *want* to have it – she couldn't even think of it as a baby, only as a thing, an alien being, a tiny stranger that had invaded her, that was not part of her own self, not really anything to do with her at all, just a horrible thing like a tumour that had taken root deep inside her and was growing each week, each day, each moment. Soon it would take her over completely. But now Mum was saying she wasn't going to have it and life would return to normal. Mum would sort it all out. She'd be safe. She'd get her life back and her body would be itself again.

Sapphire hadn't expected to get out of this so quickly and easily.

'You can't have it,' Jude said with decision. 'You're only fourteen.'

Sapphire wanted to jump up and give her mother a hug. But the expression on her mother's face checked her. It suggested that this was *not* going to be an easy way out.

Then Jude reached out her arms as if she was going to take Sapphire in a hug; instead she held her daughter by the shoulders, at arm's length.

'You'll just have to learn to live with it after it's done. And so will I,' said her mother. 'So will I.'

After it is gone . . . then what? Sapphire stared at the mute photo of Jeanne Moreau as if she might tell her the answer.

But before it was gone, Sapphire suddenly saw, there was the getting rid of. And how exactly did you do that?

Gilbert Lemon took the long way home, veering away from the city along the Great Western Road to the furthest edge of Hungry, where he lived. When he got to his home he didn't go inside. Instead, he sat on the scrubby patch of grass beside the caravan, trying to block out the noise of Martin, his father, clunking about in the tiny toilet, getting ready for bed.

Tonight, more than ever, Gilbert needed his own space. The only place to get that was outside the caravan, not inside, with Dad fiddling about. He needed his father to hurry up and settle down in bed so that Gilbert could go over and over, as many times as he wanted, what had happened tonight with the girl. He wouldn't let himself think of her until all the teeth brushing and gargling and toilet flushing had stopped, until everything fell still and the night felt like his own.

The caravan door opened and light spilled out, all over Gilbert's back. He wriggled, wanting to shake it off, needing the dark. He could hear his dad still brushing his teeth in the doorway.

'Coming in?' Martin burbled through a mouthful of froth.

'It's too hot in there,' said Gilbert, keeping his back to the caravan. 'Give me ten minutes.'

Though he'd be out here for hours, he knew. But it *was* too hot in the caravan. Its thin walls gave no shelter from the heat. They seemed to box it in and condense it.

'Lock up behind you then,' Martin frothed. But he still hovered in the doorway. Gilbert heard the tooth brushing take on a hollow tone as Dad craned his head back, reaching his back teeth as he squinted up at the sky. 'Nice night for moon-watching, eh?'

Gilbert nodded his head. He was trying not to snap. What did he have to do to get some peace?

Luckily, his father went back inside and Gilbert could hear him humming as he rinsed out his toothpastey mouth. But he'd be back, Gilbert knew. Any minute now he'd want to start up on Ulysses. His saxophone.

Most nights, however late Gilbert came home, that's what happened. They didn't talk too much, him and Dad; instead they sat under the stars, Gilbert on the grass with his thoughts and Dad on the steps of the caravan playing long, lonely sonatas that sounded as if they were made of the blue winds of space.

Most nights, Gilbert quite liked it. But not on moon nights, and not tonight.

'There she is,' Martin announced from the doorway. 'Rising up over Hungry Hill.'

And there she was, a curving slice of apricot moon, sliding from up behind the silhouette of Hunger Home. Gilbert's heart beat harder as the moon revealed the dark shape of the tower.

'Puts me in the mood for some soul,' said Martin. 'I'll get Ulysses out, eh?'

'Go to bed, Dad.'

It came out gentler than he felt, gentle enough.

'All right, son. I'll leave you in peace.' Martin glossed over the rebuff, but there was an edge of worry in his voice.

Gilbert heard it but put it to the back of his mind, as he had been doing all summer. His father was worried about him, he knew, but it was unlikely that he would confront him because Martin didn't like confrontation. He avoided it. That was just the way he was, a fact that made life easy and hard for Gilbert in equal measure.

The caravan door shut with a click and now, at last, Gilbert's thoughts were his own.

'*I have to talk to you.*' That was what she'd whispered and her words had made a pain in his heart.

'*I don't know what to say. I thought maybe you wouldn't want to know me. It was only yesterday I really knew for sure. That's why I never said anything before.*'

She was just a darkness, a silhouette. He couldn't see her face or her eyes, couldn't see her at all really, but she was beautiful, the silhouette of her body backlit by the spotlights on the grass, the edges of her hair glistening and alive.

At first he was plain shocked. And still full of nervous energy from his dash over the wall. In his bedazzlement, he took her for something magical, maybe a wood sprite that lived in the grounds. She didn't look real at all, so small and waifish, surrounded by light that seemed to burst from her skin.

When he saw her run away into Hunger Home and, minutes later, saw lamplight fill the window of the tower room at the very top, he imagined her like Rapunzel with the castle as her prison. Her voice had been so soft and hesitant that he hadn't made out exactly what she said, but he knew fear when he heard it.

She was in trouble, and scared.

Gilbert knew about that. He had a big, empty space inside that he had never been able to fill. That empty space was where he nestled his thoughts about the girl. What scared her? What had happened to her? Her voice had been so low he had to strain to hear.

She had sought him out in his hiding place in the

trees. She had come to him. Usually, girls looked through him as if he were invisible, if they looked his way at all.

But *she* knew about him. She knew his secret. Knew for sure, she said. Gilbert thought about that and discovered he was glad.

He reimagined the girl and her low, scared voice, speaking just to him, alone, in the darkness of the trees. Only one other thing ever filled his whole body, from head to toes, with such a dangerous rush.

A ripe apricot moon had risen clear over Hunger Home and its tower. For the first time since he was five years old, Gilbert Lemon gazed up at the moon and didn't look away.

Termination. She'd heard the word. It meant the end of something, like the last stop on the bus.

Abortion. That was the other word. It meant putting a stop to something that was going wrong. A pilot aborted take-off when an engine wasn't firing properly.

Sapphire supposed there must be pills that Mum could get her, so that she wouldn't have to have anything to do with hospitals and the kinds of things she'd heard lurid snatches about in the school playground, but never really listened to; she hadn't wanted to hear.

Sapphire sat down on the edge of the bath. The bathroom door was bolted so that she could think in peace.

She thought of the morning-after pill that she never had the nerve to buy; never seriously thought of buying because that would have meant admitting to herself that she and Jay were doing something that might end up, well, like this. If there was a morning-after pill, then wouldn't there be something similar for unwanted pregnancies? Something simple and safe and painless.

But how exactly did it work? It couldn't be too difficult,

surely. She could only be about three months' pregnant, she guessed. The thing inside her would be tiny, wouldn't it? The size of a baked bean or a jelly baby. She'd read that somewhere. Surely she'd be able to get rid of that without too much trouble. It wouldn't be much different from a period. Maybe it just . . . dissolved.

But Sapphire's stomach turned as she remembered her mother's face; her expression seemed to confirm the horrible playground gossip.

Maybe it wouldn't be easy. Maybe it would be terrible.

It wasn't a baked bean or a jelly baby. She wasn't really thinking about the tiny thing inside her. She hadn't thought about it once. Only about herself. And she was going to wipe it out, this *thing*, as she called it, before she could let herself think of what it really was – the tiniest scrap of human life, the start of a baby, that she had made with Jay.

And Jay – what about him?

She couldn't really blame him. Not any more than herself. They'd managed to pretend to each other that because they never *meant* things to get out of hand, that somehow nothing really had happened. If they thought like that, if they never actually planned to have sex, then they never had to deal with it beforehand.

It just kept 'happening', unexpectedly.

They had both been stupid so it didn't seem fair that only she had ended up in this horrific mess. All Sapphire had to do was breathe his name and Jay would be dragged into it too. Sapphire thought of Mrs Webb, Jay's mother. A brisk, kind woman, always busy – rushing out to work, making frantic phone calls while cooking or loading the dishwasher or polishing the many windows and varnished wood floors of Jay's plush villa. It was taken for granted that Jay, like Mrs Webb, his father and older brother, would go to university and study accountancy then join the family firm. Jay didn't question this – the Webbs were a family of accountants and his secure vision of his future slotted in smoothly with theirs.

Mrs Webb would be furious if she knew Sapphire was pregnant. Sapphire imagined the woman's distracted, friendly face turn sharp and angry at the news. There would be absolutely no question of Sapphire having the baby if Jay's mother and Jude got together.

So there was really no point in involving her or Jay, was there?

Anyway, she didn't want Jay to know. Not now. Not after she'd seen him with Grace on Hungry Hill.

After it is gone . . . once it was gone, no one would ever know it had been there.

Except her. And Mum. And Dad. How would they feel about her once it was all over? It was their grandchild she was destroying. Sapphire shuddered at the incredible thought. Then shuddered again.

How would she feel about herself?

The life you had is nothing, Jeanne Moreau reminded her from the back of the bathroom door. *It is the life you have that is important*.

'Ssh,' Sapphire told the photo but the words rang true.

Now that Mum and Dad knew, it was beginning to feel real. For the first time, what it meant hit home.

This was a battle for survival. Her life against the new one growing inside her. The life she had was nothing. It was gone. Her life now included the life of a baby that only this minute – ironically, just as Mum had insisted she wasn't to have it – Sapphire was beginning to believe in at last.

*

As soon as he woke next morning, Gilbert Lemon came to his senses.

That was no wood sprite last night. No Rapunzel either. It was Sapphire Dean.

He'd seen her at school. Pretty and popular, she was the kind of girl that would never talk to a boy like him, if she ever noticed him at all. Sapphire Dean was the only person he knew in Hungry, apart from himself, who didn't live in a house of their own. But where he lived in a cramped caravan, she lived in the castle-like mansion of Hunger Home.

Outside his life with his father in the caravan, Gilbert lived like a shadow, which made all sorts of things possible.

There was so much about himself that Gilbert didn't understand. Why had he no mother? Why did he live in a caravan on the edge of Hungry when other people lived in houses? Why was his life so different?

In a place like Hungry, it was dangerous to be different. People didn't like it. In Hungry, everyone did much the same as everyone else. Being different was offensive. You could see that in people's eyes.

And Gilbert had become exactly that – dangerous and offensive. Only no one knew. No one at all. That was the best bit. Because no one took any notice of a boy who knew how to be as silent and still as a shadow under a tree.

Gilbert told himself stories to make sense of all the things he couldn't understand. What else could he do? His father was the only one in the world who could tell Gilbert his true story, but he wouldn't – the once or twice Gilbert had tried to make him, he had been met with a wall of saxophone noise. The past was closed to him, said the sax. They were here, this is how it was, and that was that. Gilbert was left to fill in the blanks with his own imaginings.

So he did. And that was how his mother ended up on the dark side of the moon.

Dad wanted him to think his mother was dead. He hadn't ever said so – Gilbert just knew. But he also knew that she wasn't dead.

Locked away in a dark corner of Gilbert's mind was a clue.

It was the memory of a night, long ago, when he was still little enough to sleep with the back of a chair pushed against his bed to stop him falling out. Mum was sitting on the arm of the chair with her coat on and Gilbert could see the the shine of tears on her face, even though she had half-turned her face away from the light in the hall.

'Will the fairy come tonight?' he'd asked. He was so young that he was more concerned with the tooth that had just fallen out than by his mother crying.

She had to go away, she said. She didn't want to leave him, *didn't* want to at all, but she had to go, just had to.

'Go where?' Gilbert had asked, never suspecting she meant forever, that she would never come back, that this was his last moment with her.

They had lived in a house then, like ordinary people, and Mum had lifted an edge of the curtain and looked out at the moon. It was a thin crescent, as if someone had drawn a perfect curve in the sky with a silver pen. You could see the round circle of the rest of the moon, filled with darkness – the dark side of the moon. And leading right up to the moon was a silver path. The path stretched up from the earth towards the moon.

Gilbert heard his mother sob. He never forgot that sound.

'I'll come back one day. I promise I will.'

She'd grabbed him in a quick, hard hug, then left.

She hadn't come back, though Gilbert never quite stopped hoping and believing in her promise that she would.

From the very next day, Dad acted as if she'd never existed. All Gilbert could do was to make up a story to explain to himself what had happened to her, where she had gone. The story was all he had to fill in the blank space where his mother used to be.

He remembered a bedtime story she liked to tell him about how all the lost and missing things in the world – odd socks and gloves and shoes, bits of jewellery, watches full of wasted time and the rusted clasps of broken promises – all ended up in a great crater on the dark side of the moon. So when she disappeared and didn't return, Gilbert had fretted that that's where his mother must be.

Somehow, she had ended up among all the lost and missing things on the dark side of the moon where he couldn't see her, no matter how hard he tried. That was why she'd looked up at the moon like that and cried, just before she'd left. She'd been torn away from him by some moon-power that was stronger than gravity, stronger even than her love for him, and had stepped out of her life with him and on to the silver path in the sky.

Even now, twelve years later, when he should have been far too old for fairy stories, Gilbert half-imagined her up there whenever he looked at the moon.

So he tried not to look.

And then, this summer, he kept hearing a song. They'd been playing it on the radio non-stop. Every time he heard the song about a girl who left everything to live up on the moon and explore the stars, he seemed to glimpse his mother with the blue winds of space at her back, the Milky Way at her feet and drops of Jupiter in her hair; just like the girl in the song. The more he heard it, the more he began – for the first time in his life – to understand what might have made his mother go.

And he found that he was in the song too, demanding to know if she'd missed him while she'd gone looking for herself among the stars.

Why had she not taken him? Maybe that was why he lived like a shadow on the edges of this world, jealous of the life she'd chosen over him and his dad. He had been left behind in the wrong life.

Rage at his abandonment was at the root of his dangerous games. He knew that. It had begun soon after she'd left. Then, it had just been a little boy's game. Matches, leaves and paper. Kids' stuff.

Not now.

She should never have promised to come back. That had made it worse. *A promise is nothing until it's delivered.* He'd read that on a lorry once and it was true.

The night his mother left had been full of the sound of breaking glass. When the door banged shut, the force of it shook the house. Gilbert jumped up from where he was huddled under the bedclothes to look out of his window. He saw his mother get into a car and go. There were shards of broken moonlight all over the street. Tears of fright stung his eyes and made the sky seem full of smashed stars. And in the morning, a carpet of crystal covered the kitchen floor.

Dad had smashed up the house.

Why? Gilbert asked. Why had she gone away?

He never got an answer. And he'd never been able to find out because after that night he had not been allowed to mention her, ever again. It was as if she'd never existed at all. As if Gilbert and his father had always lived without her, and one day Dad had just dreamed himself up a son.

When Dad had bundled him into a van with all their belongings, saying they were going to have a new life in a place called Hungry, Gilbert had felt guilty. He'd overheard the phone call where Dad had lost his job as a mechanic. The reason he'd lost it, Gilbert knew, from the argument he'd overheard, was because his father kept sneaking away early to see to him after school and had taken time off to look after him when he was ill.

They were told there was accommodation with the new job, running a petrol station on the outskirts of Hungry. There was. It turned out to be a caravan on a wasteland.

'This is an adventure,' said Dad, trying to be upbeat, as they settled in. And little Gilbert felt it was. 'We won't always be here,' Dad promised. 'We'll find a real house soon.'

But there were no houses in Hungry that they could afford, and no jobs anywhere for a fifty-year-old man, it seemed. So here they were, living in a caravan on a bleak wasteland on the edge of Hungry.

And now, unexpectedly, Sapphire Dean had come into his life. She might not be a sprite or a princess in a castle but there was magic in her all right, because she'd cast some strange spell upon him.

Until last night, Gilbert had never been able to look at the moon without the kind of pain that could burn a person up, from the inside out.

'Where does she think she's going?' Boris demanded.

It was awful. Ever since last night her father had hardly

been able to look at her, thought Sapphire. Now he was speaking about her as if she wasn't there.

'Just out,' said Sapphire.

'Oh, no she's not. She's going nowhere. And certainly not looking like that.'

Again, he ignored her and talked over her head.

'Looking like what?' asked Jude.

'Half-naked and with all that muck on her face.'

'It's just a bit of eyeshadow and lipgloss,' Sapphire muttered. She'd been wearing it all summer and he'd never bothered before. 'Everyone's wearing shorts and crop tops in this heat.'

'And is *everyone* pregnant?'

Now he turned to her, and Sapphire wished he hadn't. His face, as his eyes flicked from her forehead to her ear to her feet, as if trying to avoid contact with her eyes or her body, made her feel hollow inside.

'Well, I don't see what difference it all makes now,' said Jude with a sigh. She rubbed her tense forehead with the heel of her hand. 'I don't see why she can't go out.'

'I want her kept indoors,' said Boris, speaking in the slow and overly measured tones he used with the most demanding or befuddled old folk. 'I don't want her hanging about the streets, getting into any more trouble than she's already in. And I don't want the whole of Hungry knowing about this – at least not until they have to. And I definitely do not want her going about looking like *that* any more.'

Sapphire blushed bright red. Up till now, Dad had only ever told her she was beautiful. Well, whenever he had time to look at her, he did. He still sometimes called her his Sapphire jewel, just as he'd done when she was little and, though she'd scoff at the name, it still made her feel special. Now, though she looked exactly the same as yesterday, she had become someone quite different in his eyes. She looked like *that*, he said, and she knew what *that* meant. Yet she looked no different from any of her friends.

'Boris, the damage is already done. What trouble can she get into now? I don't see that anyone needs to know anything about this, ever. We can sort it all out, maybe even before school starts, and no one will know at all. We've got a doctor's appointment tomorrow—'

'What do you mean, "sort it all out"?' Dad interrupted. 'Sort out what? How long what'll take?'

He stared at Mum, his brow crinkling.

'Well, your daughter is fourteen years old—'

'As you've said a thousand times—'

'So obviously she can't have a baby.'

'Obviously? Can't? She was old enough to conceive it.' Boris's bewilderment cleared into outrage. 'Jude, don't you dare!' he exploded.

'Don't I dare what? I'm her mother. She's fourteen. What do you expect me to do?'

'Not that. That I *will not* let you do, Jude. It's murder. You can't murder your own flesh and blood,' his voice shook with revulsion, 'when we're perfectly capable of looking after it.'

'Who is?' Jude was scathing. 'I know perfectly well who'll be stuck looking after it – me!'

'I could never live with the fact that I let my daughter abort her own child,' said Boris.

'And I couldn't live with the fact that I let my child abort her own life – and land me with the responsibility of *another* child I didn't plan on having,' shouted Jude. 'Will I never be free?'

One of them wouldn't forgive her, Sapphire saw, whatever she did.

And she could only wonder at that last comment of her mother's. Had she not wanted Gretel? Or any of them?

'There's a boy involved in this.' Boris changed tack. 'I want the boy's name.'

'As if that matters,' muttered Jude.

'It matters to *me*,' said Boris.

Sapphire backed out of the room.

'It doesn't matter!' she heard Jude yell back. 'He's not going to marry her, Boris. He'll only be a schoolboy and she's still a child.'

'I won't let you—'

'So what do *you* suggest,' Jude yelled over him, 'that your FOURTEEN-YEAR-OLD pregnant daughter does? If she has this baby her life's over – and I know about that, don't I!'

'I suggest,' Boris muttered, 'that you keep your voice down. The whole of Hungry must have heard you by now.'

Sapphire heard no more. She was out of the room, down the stairs and racing through the grounds of Hunger Home and on her way to the bus stop to catch the next bus into the city before they even noticed she was gone.

The Atlantic wind carried the city's dust into the suburbs. Even on the hottest nights of the heatwave, a sudden warm gust would sigh through the streets and bring with it the faint, chaotic odour of the city mixed with the even more distant scent of the ocean and the dry, fragrant sea grasses that fringed a hundred miles of western shore.

The wisp woman knew those heady scents. They had led, in a roundabout way, to here and now, standing at this bus stop on her twilight watch after her cleaning shift at Hunger Home.

She leaned against the wall of the bus shelter. It didn't

matter if she was tired out. All that mattered was that she would see him, if she waited long enough. Hunger Home was where the boy ran to, as if he ran for the safety of his own home.

The thought filled the woman with joy. So strange, wasn't it, that he ran to the very place that she lived. It was almost as if he knew.

But he didn't.

And now here he was. She watched the boy race across the road and up along the pavement towards Hunger Home, towards herself.

Without moving, the woman came alive.

Without seeing her, the boy sprang up on to the wall, right behind the bus shelter where she stood, and vaulted over into the grounds. For no more than a second she had a glimpse of his face as he glanced back, checking for pursuers.

Beyond the drum of her heart, she heard the sirens. It took exactly seven and a half minutes for the fire engines to roar along the Great Western Road.

Out of the corner of her eye, she registered one red flash then another turn into an avenue just within sight of the bus shelter. Once she was sure they were out of the way, and that no one was around, the woman slid out of the bus shelter and pushed through the bushes and thorny brambles to put her hands on the spot the boy's hands had touched when he vaulted over the wall.

'*As I burned life*,' she murmured, remembering the line from her special poem. And sighed, because she understood.

Sapphire sat waiting at a secluded table in the corner of Di Maggio's, the pizzeria where Miranda worked the whole summer to boost the meagre funds she had to live on all year as a student. These days, Sapphire saw hardly anything of her sister. Miranda spent most of her time at a friend's flat in the university quarter of the city. The flat was within walking distance of Di Maggio's and the university where Miranda was studying for a law degree. Evenings and weekends Miranda served up pizzas, then walked round the corner to spend the night on her friend Louise's sofa bed. The rest of her time was spent in cafes that buzzed with life from early morning till late at night in the streets around the university.

Now, she was only home on Sundays. It had taken Miranda's absence for Sapphire to realize that she missed having her sister around. She missed being able to steal her clothes and make-up. She missed her sister's clever, sharp, wicked tongue. She even missed fighting with her.

Sapphire yawned and stared at the stylish black-and-white photos of Hollywood film stars that were scattered all over the scarlet-painted walls of the pizzeria. Mum's photo of Jeanne Moreau would fit in perfectly. It had the same subtle glamour as the photo of Greta Garbo that hung right above her table. For the first time, with that unsettling outburst of her mother's about her own unwanted pregnancies echoing in her head, Sapphire had an uneasy sense of why her mother sat in the cupboard so many nights with a bottle of gin. Maybe she could have had an amazing career as a photographer, with her photos hung on restaurant walls all over the world – if she hadn't married Dad and had Sapphire and her sisters.

Instead, Mum spent half her life seeing to the needs of Hunger Home's old people, and the other half seeing to the needs of her own family. Any time left over, and there wasn't much, she spent in her den.

The photo above a nearby table showed a couple running, hand in hand, across a cityscape busy with skyscrapers. They were in love with each other, you could see that in the way their bodies were crushed together, their hands clasped, and in the look of bliss on their faces. And yet they looked as if at any moment they might pull apart and dash off in completely different directions because – Sapphire wasn't sure how she knew this, but she did – they were even more in love with their own lives.

Why had Mum chosen the life she had, when she could have had a career taking photos like that? What would have happened if she had?

Sapphire would not have been born, that's what. She, Miranda and Gretel would not exist.

Sapphire felt blank and slightly queasy as she tried to imagine this. She had drunk as many Cokes as she could stomach while she waited for Miranda to finish her shift – so many that all the sugar and caffeine were starting to make her trembly and sick, adding to her queasiness. She caught herself wondering if the baby inside got the shakes from too many Cokes, then killed the thought. It wasn't a baby. It was nothing, just a slug-like thing the size of a button or a bean. It couldn't think or feel, could it? It didn't really exist at all.

Miranda was weaving through the tables, dancing to the soul soundtrack. The corners of the red-checked paper tablecloths flapped a tiny Mexican wave when she passed. She presented menus to the couple at a table near to Sapphire's with a graceful flourish.

'Dessert? I can recommend the hot fudge cake. Gorgeous,' Miranda urged the couple with a sweet smile.

Liar, thought Sapphire. Miranda hadn't let anything fattening pass her lips in years.

'Want an ice cream?' Miranda mouthed the words at her.

Sapphire shook her head.

'Thought you finished at seven,' she mouthed back.

Miranda shrugged. She tucked her blouse into her tight black trousers and flicked her sleek, dark hair over her shoulder like a girl in a shampoo ad, as she brushed past Sapphire's table. 'Won't be long, I'm just waiting for this couple to finish up. TV people,' she whispered in Sapphire's ear and grinned. 'Loaded. Good tips.' She frowned and suddenly lapsed into big-sisterhood. 'How did you get here anyway? Do Mum and Dad know you're here?'

'Bus, yeah, 'course,' lied Sapphire, glancing behind and recognizing the woman's face from TV news. 'Shut up, Miranda, I'm not a kid.'

Miranda raised an eyebrow in disagreement. She danced off back through the tables, looking so free and at ease in herself, Sapphire noted enviously, just like Jay was in his body. For a while now, even before the pregnancy, her body had often felt like it wasn't altogether hers. It had become something boys and men had begun to notice and appraise, and though that was exciting, it felt strange and awkward too. These days, she was always over-conscious of how she looked, as if she'd bought a great new outfit but didn't feel entirely at ease in it.

Behind the bar Joe, the pizzeria manager, slid his eyes over Miranda for the umpteenth time. Sapphire had been watching him eyeing her sister, wondering if he really thought he was in with a chance. He couldn't be serious. He was ancient. About the same age as their dad. Anyway, Miranda seemed oblivious, too wrapped up in herself and the music to notice.

But now, as she danced up to the bar to collect some

drinks, Miranda seemed all of a sudden to feel the weight of Joe's gaze. Her dance stopped dead and when she turned back round with the tray of drinks her cheeks were flushed. As she took the drinks over to a table, Miranda balanced the tray on one hand and surreptitiously fastened the top buttons on her white blouse. She looked awkward, out of sorts.

Sapphire's heart sank. If her clever, gorgeous, eighteen-year-old sister, who had sailed through school and right out of Hungry with such flair and confidence, hadn't worked out how to deal with the world, then what chance did Sapphire have?

None now.

'So what's up? Exactly why are you here?' Miranda took out her note pad and pretended to be writing down an order. 'Missing your beloved big sister, are you? Don't think so,' she answered before Sapphire could respond. 'There was a message from Mum on the answering machine last night when I got home. I gather you've done something un*speak*able – though I couldn't make out exactly what Mum was ranting about.'

Sapphire had decided there was only one way to tell Miranda. It had to be in public so that she wouldn't go berserk and thump her.

'I'm in big trouble.'

Miranda flicked her eyes heavenwards. 'I'd sussed that from the answering machine.' She glanced at her watch. 'Well, I'm near enough finished.' With a big-sister sigh, she sat down and looked at Sapphire. 'So what've you done?'

She thinks I'm a kid, thought Sapphire, irritated. Well, she won't in a minute.

All the same, it wasn't easy to get the words out.

'I'm – I'm . . .'

'What? Oh, come on, Sapphire.'

'I'm pregnant.'

'Don't be silly.'

'I am.'

'Listen, at your age, your period might not always be—'

'I'm pregnant, Miranda.'

Her tone of voice, definite and suddenly mature, even to Sapphire's own ears, made her sister blink.

'Pregnant?' Miranda sat back in her seat. She looked as if she was going to be sick. 'Oh, my god. Sapphire, you can't be.'

'Well, I am.'

'You – you *know* this? It's confirmed?'

Sapphire nodded.

'I did a test. The predictor stick you buy in the chemist.'

Miranda stared for long, long moments. Then she turned her head away.

'But that's – that's horrible. It's the worst thing I can imagine. Oh my God. I'd rather *die* than get pregnant. I'd rather be run over by a bus.'

Sapphire gulped.

'It's not the end of the world,' she said, trying to believe it, but her voice shook because it felt as if it was. 'It – it happens all the time. Thousands of schoolgirls get pregnant every year. It's always in the papers.'

'But it's not a very smart idea, is it?' Suddenly Miranda was sharp as ever, forgetting they were sitting at a table in Di Maggio's near the TV couple. 'You're supposed to make sure *you're* not one of them. Why didn't you? You've been taught all about contraception in school.'

'No. We haven't done it yet,' said Sapphire. 'We get that next year.'

Miranda closed her eyes and cursed under her breath.

She raked her hair back from her face with her hands, distraught.

'There's no excuse. There isn't. You're not stupid. You can think. All the information, all the stuff is out there. You could have got a contraceptive from – well, from anywhere. God, Sapphire! You're just a kiddie. What have you done?'

Miranda's eyes filled up. To stop herself from crying, Sapphire bit her lip and fixed her mind on Mum's secret plan.

'I mean, there's no excuse. We've had *every* advantage in life.' Miranda wiped her eyes and began to lecture. 'Good family, good school, nice friends. You're bright, educated, both parents working, nuclear family intact, we live in a nice area with very little crime—'

'What about the firebug?' Sapphire cut in, but she felt increasingly listless.

'That's a blip,' said Miranda. 'And it'll be a boy. Probably someone from outside Hungry. The fact is that *girls* like us don't muck up. We just don't. We've had all the advantages in life anyone could have. What's your excuse?'

Sapphire clenched her fists. And then she knew what to say. She knew how to annoy Miranda.

'I don't know. Something came over me. It just happened . . . I didn't mean to . . . wasn't really sure what I was doing . . .'

Lies. All lies.

The words spilled out easily and she recognized them. They were straight out of the romantic novels some of the old women read to fill their days in Hunger Home. Often, when bored, Sapphire would pick up a paperback in the reading room and sit up half the night racing through it.

'Were you drunk?' asked Miranda. Her brow crinkled.

She was trying desperately to make some kind of sense of her young sister's apparent senselessness. 'Why – I mean, *why* didn't you take precautions? You could have walked into a chemist or a cafe—'

'In Hungry?' said Sapphire. 'There aren't any cafes and Mum would know about it in five minutes if I went into the chemist.'

'Then you could have jumped on a bus like you just did and found a cafe or a chemist here – don't tell me you're so clueless you couldn't do that.'

Miranda was right, of course.

'I – I didn't like to,' Sapphire admitted.

'You didn't *like* to,' Miranda mimicked. 'Well, do you *like* being pregnant?'

'But we were really careful!' Sapphire protested. 'We were. I made sure we only ever did anything in the safe time. That's why I don't know—'

Sapphire stopped, realizing that she had been lying to herself about not meaning to have sex with Jay. It hadn't 'just happened', because each time she had planned out when she thought it would be safe.

'*What* safe time?' Miranda asked warily.

'You know, just after your period. Emma read somewhere that—'

Miranda exploded. 'Don't tell me you're stupid enough to believe playground gossip!'

'No,' insisted Sapphire. 'Emma was sure.'

Miranda closed her eyes and sighed. 'I think events have proved Emma wrong, don't you?'

A great tremble ran right through Sapphire. Had Emma got it wrong? She saw from the look on her sister's face that Emma had. But Emma's mum was a doctor and Emma was always picking up interesting snippets from her medical magazines, so Sapphire had never thought to question. But now she began to wonder if it *was* Emma who'd got it wrong. Maybe Emma had told her the right thing and she'd remembered it wrong. Like Chinese Whispers, the facts had somehow become distorted along the line.

Jay hadn't questioned it either. He'd taken her word for it. At least – Sapphire forced herself to remember more precisely – he had taken her unspoken assurance that it would be fine, that she had it all sorted when the fact was she felt too awkward to bring the subject up. It would have spoiled everything, somehow. It had been much easier just to put such practicalities out of her mind and do what her body told her was right.

So Jay was hardly to blame, was he? Or was he? But it wasn't Jay who'd ended up pregnant.

'So you had sex at a time of the month when you were *likely* to get pregnant,' said Miranda, enunciating carefully to let every word hit home. 'And you thought you were being careful.'

Sapphire bit her lip again as she remembered lying out in the darkness of Hungry Hill with Jay, when all the others had gone home, convincing herself that there was hardly any risk, that she'd get away with it. Mum and Dad wouldn't notice if she sneaked in late, and she just knew that nothing bad would happen, not to her.

'Oh, Sapphire.' Miranda put her head in her hands. 'Not clever.'

The whoosh of the coffee machine at the bar filled a long, miserable silence.

'Who is he, then – this schoolboy Casanova of yours?' Miranda demanded at last.

'Maybe I'm not clever like you, Miranda,' Sapphire burst out, to avoid answering that question, wanting to hit back.

'You're *so* smart and clever but you don't – well, you don't exactly live, do you? You don't know how to have fun. You just study and serve up pizza—'

'And this is your idea of fun? Fourteen and pregnant – that's really living, Sapphire, real fun.' Miranda drummed her fingers on the table. 'I just don't understand how you could be so st—' She glanced at Sapphire and bit her lip to stop the word slipping out.

Sapphire felt something rise inside her. Something hot and unbearable. The feeling erupted from her in burning tears. 'I don't know why either! I felt like it! I just *felt* like it!'

Miranda's head twitched as she suddenly remembered the TV couple at the nearby table. They were sitting in silence, pretending to be studying the dessert menu that Miranda had handed them a good ten minutes before. They were obviously listening to every word.

'Feelings are not there to be followed,' Miranda hissed.

'Why?' Sapphire retreated into sullen childishness.

'Because,' Miranda responded, 'this is where it gets you. You control your feelings; they don't control you. Where would the world be if everyone just acted on their feelings? We'd all be at war—'

Sapphire made a yawning noise. She caught the eye of the TV woman for a second. 'Lots of the world *is* at war.'

'Exactly,' snapped Miranda. 'So you keep a grip of yourself and think of your future. You don't do what you *feel* like and wreck it.' Miranda was whispering but she had a disconnected, inward expression on her face and Sapphire knew she was really talking to herself now. 'Sometimes, to get to where you want to go, you have to switch off your feelings or they'd lead you astray.'

Sapphire watched the TV woman delve into a chunk of

fudge cake that another waitress had delivered. They'd given up waiting for Miranda to take their order. She'd have lost her tip now. The woman closed her eyes for a second as she took a spoonful of hot chocolate fudge. 'Shouldn't be eating this but what the hell, sometimes you've got to live,' Sapphire heard her laugh softly to her partner, as she lifted a dripping spoonful to his mouth.

Sapphire slumped back in her chair and looked at her sister, who was now sunk in her own thoughts. Miranda was the kind of girl she'd never be. Exam-clever, but smart too. And good-looking in a classy, self-assured way. Miranda and Grace, she saw, were both of a kind. In fact, thought Sapphire, Grace would have been a more likely sister for Miranda. Except Miranda would have hated that. Too much competition.

But they were the sisters under the skin, those two. They had it all and they knew it. They knew what they were: perfect. They just loved themselves, you could see it. Chocolate girls – that's what Emma called girls like Miranda and Grace. Because, she reckoned, they loved themselves so much that if they were chocolate, they'd eat themselves right up.

Sapphire glanced over her sister's smooth hair and skin, the shiny nails that matched her lipgloss, the spotless white blouse tucked into tight black jeans that discreetly showed off her neat body. What would it be like to love everything about yourself? Sapphire knew she was pretty enough, yet beside girls like Miranda and Grace she felt full of flaws – suddenly she became aware of her broken nails, hair that could never make up its mind if it was straight or curly, and that tiny bump on her nose where she'd once fallen off her bike. As for her body, well, it was fine; yet somehow, next to theirs, it suddenly felt inadequate.

But those nights all alone with Jay up on Hungry Hill once everyone else had gone home, she had felt different then. Special, really special. Maybe it was the cover of darkness, but Jay hadn't seemed to notice any flaws. She'd felt perfect then. As perfect as the ultimate chocolate girl. And he'd acted as if she was, as if he wanted to eat her all up.

Sapphire caught her breath as she remembered, in a feeling that swept her from head to foot and turned her inside out, the pulsing excitement of those nights. She had loved being in her body then. It was thrilling, exhilarating. It was the way she used to feel when she was younger and she'd race down Hungry Hill, yelling into the wind, or when she'd cycle round and round the streets as fast as she could go. She hadn't felt so free and full of her own power for ages.

She'd wanted to hold on to that feeling.

'Just keep a grip,' Miranda murmured. 'Put a stop on your feelings.'

'I don't want to. I like my feelings.'

Even to herself Sapphire sounded sulkily childish. But what Miranda was saying shocked her. Was that what growing up meant – your feelings had to stop?

'Sometimes you just have to,' said Miranda, snapping out of herself and back into the moment. 'I mean, it's your stupid feelings that got you into this mess. I could easily have mucked up, loads of times. But you have to be smart. Boys are useless about things like that, so we have to be smart. It's our lives that get ruined if we don't, not theirs. That's why girls are more mature, because you have to be. It's up to you not to get yourself pregnant.' Miranda flicked her sleek hair over her shoulder and looked away from her sister and sighed. 'But it's too late. You've already mucked up.'

Sapphire felt more tears, sharp ones like tiny thorns, prickle her eyes.

Miranda flicked her hair again.

'I didn't actually get *myself* pregnant,' Sapphire burst out. And stopped, too late.

Miranda was right in there. 'So who's the father?' She gave a soft laugh and shook her head. 'The father. It's unbelievable. Pitiful.'

Sapphire let her hair fall over her face and sat silent and sullen.

'Oh, don't be stupid,' said Miranda, sighing. 'Just tell me.'

'If you call me stupid once more I'll thump you,' hissed Sapphire. 'I will.'

'Very mature.'

'Well, I'm *not* mature,' exploded Sapphire. 'I'm just a *stupid*, clueless, fourteen-year-old. But don't worry, Miranda, I'll be fine. I've to get rid of it – the baby. Mum said so. She said I can.'

Miranda stared and the look on her face gratified Sapphire's battered sense of self. Because the look on Miranda's face wasn't one you gave to a child or stupid young sister. It was the expression of one woman out-manoeuvred by another. And there was just a ripple of something else – not envy, but the look Miranda might have if, while gliding confidently through the tables carrying a tray of pizzas, Sapphire had stuck out her leg and tripped her up. It was an awkward, out-of-sorts look like the one she'd had when Joe threatened her centre of balance with his leering eyes.

For the first time in Miranda's life her little sister had overtaken her. She was way ahead of her in the world. Not only that, Sapphire was out on her own, in a murky, dangerous place where a girl from Hungry was never supposed to be.

Sapphire felt a strange, bittersweet triumph as she stood up to leave her sister who was, for once, right out of her depth.

In the time it took the bus to travel half of the long, straight arm of the Great Western Road that took her out of the city and back into the suburbs, Sapphire had relived the whole history of herself and Jay, and discovered something incredible.

She didn't love him.

She hadn't slept with him because she had loved him. It had been nothing to do with loving him. Or about him loving her. His wanting her had been a thrill. It had made her feel like the most powerful person in the world. And she had fallen in love with that feeling. Not with him.

There had been just a second to choose on that too-hot, too-long afternoon in May. They chose each other and ran, as the bell rang, dodging teachers, dodging double chemistry, which they both loathed. In the empty afternoon, the streets of Hungry were so still that all Sapphire could hear, as they sneaked into Jay's house, was the beat of her own heart.

As the bus shuddered in stops and starts all along the Great Western Road, Sapphire felt the thrill of that day rebound in her body. And wanted the feeling back.

But not Jay, she didn't want him back, not now he'd ditched her for Grace. It wasn't really him she missed or wanted, after all.

And if she didn't love him, thought Sapphire, that changed everything. If she didn't love him, was her pregnancy worth anything at all?

The bus juddered to another stop. A group of teenage girls – older than Sapphire but only by a few years – stood in a gang outside a chip shop. Each one had a baby in a buggy. She studied them as the bus stopped at the lights. They seemed to have an assurance about them, those girls, as they jiggled the buggies to keep the babies happy long enough to let them chat and eat chips. They had graduated to womanhood, bypassing exams and the need to prove themselves, through having a baby. They even had their own gang, membership guaranteed by the possession of a child. They looked cool and self-possessed, all made-up and trendily dressed – but only, Sapphire saw, to stand outside the chip shop with their buggies. And if you looked close, their faces were tight with strain, shadowed with tiredness, as they each took a turn at dragging energy from a single, shared cigarette.

Miranda was right; you never saw gangs of teenage mothers in Hungry. Only in the city.

Sapphire tried to imagine herself as one of that new gang, as unlike Grace's as any could be.

No, she thought. No. Not me.

The aroma of fish and chips invaded the bus. Sweat slicked her body; the bus seats were unpleasantly sticky. Sapphire's stomach growled. She'd hardly eaten all day. She hadn't been hungry in the pizzeria; she'd been too keyed up at the thought of breaking her news to Miranda. Now she was suddenly so ravenous she could almost taste the salt and vinegar in the air. She searched the pockets of her shorts for chewing gum, anything, but there was nothing.

And suddenly her hunger plunged her back into a memory, a silly incident from years ago.

She and Miranda, aged eight and twelve, were enjoying one of their furtive searches through Mum's bedroom for lipsticks and jewellery, as they often did when left to their own devices while their parents were busy managing the Home. Miranda was reading, in a silly French accent, lines from a cache of old love letters she'd found tucked away at the back of Mum's underwear drawer – letters not from Dad, but from someone called Theo. Someone from Mum's time in Paris, guessed Miranda who, like Sapphire, had adorned herself with Mum's scarves and jewellery that were packed away in boxes at the bottom of the wardrobe.

It was here at the bottom of the wardrobe, tucked away in a bundle of scarves, that Sapphire found a box, oval-shaped, with a scarlet ribbon around it.

The box looked as if it had never been touched. Sapphire hardly hesitated before prising open the lid. There, cracked and whitened with age, was a tray of chocolates.

Sapphire breathed in the aroma: sweet and sour-edged. The date on the underside of the box lid told her the chocolates were three years older than Miranda, but she didn't care, didn't give a thought to what might befall her if she ate them, didn't even consider what would happen if she got caught. Crouched uncomfortably half-in, half-out of the wardrobe, she began stuffing them into her mouth.

Miranda was too busy trying to decipher the Parisian letters to notice. Just as Miranda was engrossed in the secrets of Mum's letters, so Sapphire was engrossed in her secret find. She kept gorging, even though the chocolates tasted slightly rancid, even when she began to feel queasy. The taste didn't matter; she'd stopped tasting them after the first handful. Now she couldn't stop herself, she was hooked on the sugar rush of each mouthful, and by the sensation of enjoying something she knew she shouldn't. Something that belonged to the grown-up world, that had a whole secret history of its own. Something that she had found all by herself, without Miranda breathing over her shoulder and spoiling it. That made it even more exciting. Even the nausea and headache that followed hadn't diminished that irresistible thrill.

Astonished, she saw that it had been just the same with Jay. It hadn't really been about him. It had been the same impulse as the one she'd felt at eight years old, gorging on forbidden chocolates in the bottom of Mum's wardrobe.

The bus jolted to a halt at the foot of Hungry Hill. Sapphire jumped off.

On the pavement, she stood for a moment. It was a strange dusk tonight, with an odd, greeny-pink light in the streets that made everything look unfamiliar. She sniffed the air. The scent of burning, yet no sign of smoke. The fire crews must have dealt with the dusk fire already. Only the scent remained.

There was just enough light to make out – if you looked closely and knew what you were looking for – the shapes of the watchers on the hill. Sapphire's heart sank. She wasn't part of that any more. She didn't want to be. Even though she didn't want Jay back, there was no way now that she could muster the courage to go up on to the hill.

Sapphire turned to push through the high rhododendron bushes behind the bus shelter, to climb over the wall into the grounds of Hunger Home, as she always did, rather than walk the long way round to the gated entrance.

A pair of eyes blinked at her from the bushes. Sapphire screamed.

The owner of the eyes screamed too and tried to push past. Sapphire stood aside, recognizing the woman. It was only the Mad Hatter. That's what the kids in Hungry called the strange woman who stood all evening at the bus stop, waiting forever, it seemed, for a bus that never came. The frail, shy, spaced-out-looking woman who lived in a room in the east wing of Hunger Home and worked there as a cleaner. Though they lived in the same place, Sapphire had never exchanged so much as a word with her; the woman kept very much to herself. She was the kind of person who could walk past you in an empty corridor and you would hardly notice she was there.

There's something odd about her eyes, Jude once said, over dinner. Medication, Boris had guessed. But it's none of our business, he added; she's a good worker.

Jude seemed to make a point of treating the woman especially kindly after that. Sapphire would see her mother stop the woman in the middle of cleaning the stairs and tell her, out of earshot of the other cleaners, to go and grab a quick cup of tea.

Sapphire had only heard her speak once, and her voice had the same faraway quality as her eyes.

'Didn't mean to scare you,' Sapphire called after the woman, as she scrambled out of the bushes and rushed off along the street.

But what had she been doing standing in a bush by the wall? Why did she hang around the bus stop? Was *she* the firebug? Sapphire suddenly wondered, as she found a foothold in the wall and pulled herself over the top. That strange woman? Surely not. But then, why not? It could be anyone.

Sapphire swung down into a clump of stinging nettles and found herself eye to eye with someone else. She almost screamed again, but stopped as she realized who it was – the boy. The one who had been in the trees. She knew it was him by the scent that hung about him. It made Sapphire think of cellars, old newspapers and cars.

Dust and petrol, that's what it was; and something more.

His scent should have told her, last night, that it wasn't Jay.

Neither spoke, only stood at a distance in the green shade of the trees.

'It was you last night, wasn't it?' said Sapphire at last.

He said nothing then nodded. A slow, hesitant nod followed by a quick, reluctant one.

'Listen, what – what I said—' Sapphire stopped. He was the only person, outside of her family, who knew her secret.

'What I said wasn't true. I'm not – not really . . . see, I thought you were someone else.'

Of course, thought Gilbert, with a sinking heart. That made sense. She hadn't really been talking to him. She'd thought he was someone else. And she *was* just a girl, nothing more, he reminded himself, though it was still hard to believe, in this magical half-light, that she wasn't the enchanted creature that his imagination had tricked him into seeing last night.

'I don't want anyone else to know what I told you,' she said. 'Please.'

Gilbert gave himself time to think.

'I wouldn't tell anyone,' he said at last, though there was nothing, in what he'd heard, to tell.

And that was true. There really was no one to tell, anyway. He hardly spoke to another soul, except his father, and usually no one spoke to him.

'Promise?'

'I don't believe in promises,' said Gilbert. 'But I said I won't.'

Sapphire heard the change in his voice. Even so, she took a step closer. His scent drew her nearer still. It puzzled her, that scent.

Gilbert took a step back. She was almost close enough

to touch. No girl had ever been this close to him before. She leaned even closer and sniffed.

'No, you can't tell,' Sapphire whispered, 'can you? Or else I'll tell on *you*.'

Firesmoke. The scent was on his skin, his hair, his clothes. He even breathed it. And mixed with that, behind the trace of dust, was the heady, chemical fume of petrol.

Gilbert sucked in a breath. She really did know. He could see it in her face. And it was his own fault. He had let himself be seen. She could ruin everything now. Even so, a thrill ran through him because he suddenly knew that if there was anyone in the world that he would want to know his secret, it was this girl.

Father Gunn entered the grounds of Hunger Home with an automatic plunge in spirit. The clang of the iron gate and the crunch of the gravel path were depressingly familiar. How many times had he clanged and crunched his way in to administer the last rites to one of the old people in Hunger Home? Father Gunn couldn't begin to remember.

Almost all of the old people had lived in Hungry their whole lives. Some families had lived there for generations. Children grew up, travelled to college or university in the city and lived at home until they found a city job that earned them enough to buy a house right back in the suburb. Then they would marry and begin a whole new Hungry generation.

But new families had multiplied much faster than the old generation was dying, and the competition for houses had become ferocious. Families grew keen to move elderly relatives into Hunger Home to free up precious housing. As a result, the Home was now full to the brim. Its waiting list stretched years into the future. Father Gunn knew for a fact that some families now urged elderly relatives to add their names to the list years in advance, sometimes as soon as they retired. And so most of the area's old people lived at the very heart of Hungry, yet set apart from everyone else, high on its central hill.

Father Gunn often wondered if he would end up in Hunger Home. Somehow, the thought made him want to get in his car and drive off out into the countryside and never come back. There was nothing terrible about the Home; as a priest, with his belief in the afterlife, he should think of it as a last resting place before his great journey into eternity.

He should, but somehow he didn't.

But this time his visit to Hunger Home was different. Father Gunn's heart lightened as he remembered why.

Today, for the first time ever, his mission was not about the old people and death. It was about young life and salvation.

For the first time in a quarter of a century, Father Gunn bounded up the stone steps of Hunger Home's pillared entrance. His spectacles glinted as he raised his face to the morning sun and squinted up towards the mansion's grand tower, where Sapphire Dean awaited his help.

'Sapphire, Father Gunn's here to see you.'

Boris stuck his head round the bedroom door. Sweat glistened on his forehead. He sounded nervy. Swiftly, he looked his daughter up and down, and his relief that she'd replaced her shorts and crop top with jeans and a loose T-shirt, as he'd urged her to, was clear.

'All right?' he asked.

Sapphire nodded, feeling sick and listless. She hadn't slept well and had spent the morning hoping that Dad was only bluffing at breakfast when he'd said the priest was coming to talk to her. Mum had been called away early to see to one of the old people, so although she was only down the corridor, Sapphire had been unable to speak to her all morning.

Sapphire picked up a brush and struggled with her hair. One side was rumpled and crinkly where she'd been lying on it all morning, sweating in the too-heavy denims and T-shirt. She smoothed the wrinkles in her clothes, thought about some lipgloss then decided against it.

Outside, in the hallway, she ran straight into Miranda.

'What're you doing here?' Sapphire felt a surge of relief. Miranda's support would be better than nothing.

Miranda grabbed her. She was breathing hard, had been running, and a sheen of sweat was loosening her make-up. Sapphire stared. Miranda never ran, never lost her cool; not these days.

'You'll never believe this,' Miranda gasped. 'After you left last night that couple – remember the TV couple? You'll never believe it!'

'Miranda—' Sapphire cut in. This really wasn't the time to hear about Miranda's career opportunities. 'Father Gunn's here. He's waiting—'

'I know. I came up the path right behind him. That's why I need to catch you now, before he corners you into anything. Sapphy, I've solved the whole problem!'

'What problem?'

Miranda gave her favourite deadpan stare. 'Ooh, let's think hard – I'll give you a hint – that little problem of your unwanted pregnancy.'

'*You've* "solved" it?' said Sapphire, drawing back warily.

'Listen,' rushed Miranda. 'That couple are desperate, absolutely desperate, for a baby. They were listening to every word last night and as soon as you'd gone they approached me. They're at their wits' end. They've spent a fortune on fertility treatment and none of it worked. They wanted to adopt, but there just aren't enough babies to go round, they said, and they're way at the bottom of the queue because of their age – she's forty-three, but you'd never think so, would you? That's the kind of life I want,' said Miranda enviously, 'brilliant career, sports car, great clothes – did you see her shoes? She's got the lot.'

Except for one thing, thought Sapphire. The thing I don't want.

She tried to picture the woman in her mind's eye, remembering her smoothly made-up face, the restless fingers on the tablecloth, her laughing, what-the-hell confidence.

'So what?' She shrugged, to annoy Miranda.

'*So*, stupid, they want a baby. And they're prepared to pay a lot for it.'

Miranda took a step back to observe her sister's response to this momentous news. When she didn't respond, Miranda prodded her. 'They were on the point of going abroad – to Romania or somewhere – to buy one there.'

'You don't buy babies,' said Sapphire.

'You're about to kill one, little sister,' Miranda retorted. Sapphire flinched and Miranda looked away. 'What I mean is – abortion is obviously the quickest solution but *this*,' she continued more gently, 'might be the clever one. Think longterm. You'll have money – ten thousand pounds, they said. That'd set you up. You could get right through uni with no debts. And that,' Miranda finished in a businesslike tone, 'was only their first offer. Remember they're desperate. We could negotiate for more. Think about it, Sapphire. Just think what this could do for your future. Instead of wrecking it, it could make it.'

For a split second, Miranda looked as if she envied Sapphire her opportunity.

Sapphire thought hard. She tried to imagine holding a tiny baby, swaddled in blankets, then handing it over to the TV woman and never seeing it again. She thought about the woman reading the evening news and Sapphire watching her, night after night, never able to stop imagining her going home to that baby, the one that was really hers. And wondering, all the time, about the baby out there, the little stranger that she'd created, and sold. Years later, on the street, when the baby was a child, or even when she was middle-aged and the baby was a grown man or woman, maybe they'd walk past each other and they'd never know.

'No,' said Sapphire.

'Sapphire, the options are abortion, formal adoption, being a teenage loser with a baby in tow or keeping your life together and giving up a baby you don't want to two respectable people who do want it – and putting your life back on track with ten thousand pounds in the bank. I know what I'd do.'

'You'll make a top lawyer, Miranda,' said Sapphire coldly. 'And anyway, how do you know they're respectable, just 'cause they've got money and they're on TV – they could be alcoholics or, well, anything.'

'Murderers even,' murmured Miranda, nastily. She always got nasty when opposed. 'Look, it's a way out of this. I wouldn't let it ground me. I intend to go as far as I can in life.'

'Where?'

'I don't necessarily mean distance, I mean in achievement.'

Sapphire gave her sister a wry look. 'You mean you want to pass all your exams and qualify as a brilliant young lawyer and earn big money so that you can buy a nice big house here in Hungry.'

She saw the smooth circular sweep that Miranda's life would take. The opposite from the downward spiral she felt herself falling into. But Miranda's kind of life had never been for her. Miranda relished the challenge of exams, whereas for Sapphire each schoolday contained something to dread.

Miranda gave Sapphire a tight smile. 'There are lots of places just as nice as Hungry.'

'Sapphire!' Dad appeared in the hallway, his face tense and white. 'In here now, please. Father Gunn is a busy man.'

'You're the one that's always going on about a woman's right to choose. What happened to that? Am I not allowed to choose?' Sapphire hissed in her sister's face, as she followed Dad into their small living room.

'You're not a woman. You're a little girl who's so stupid she's a danger to herself!' Miranda hissed back. 'You never told me whose it is yet – I suppose it's black-leather-jacket boy's?'

Sapphire punched her sister in the arm as Miranda tailed her into the living room.

'Get out or I'll kill you,' Sapphire threatened through gritted teeth.

'No chance,' said Miranda. She punched back and pushed her way in.

'Well, here you are now, young lady,' said Father Gunn, trying to remember the girl's name as she slunk into the room. A second, older girl strode into the room behind her. Her sister? But surely it must be that one – the older, confident one – who was in trouble. Father Gunn met

Miranda's cool gaze. 'Here you are,' the priest repeated, re-directing himself at Miranda.

He frowned at the girl. What *was* her name? Sandra? Sasha? The father – now what was *his* name? – had said his daughter's name just a few minutes ago. Along with the intolerable heat, the forgetfulness which came upon him more and more these days made the priest tetchy.

'What a terrible thing,' said Father Gunn, trying to nudge her name out of the annoying fogginess in his head, 'to bring upon your mother and father. And your sister.'

Miranda smirked and sat down, with a langorous crossing of her legs.

'Um, it's me,' Sapphire murmured, seeing his mistake.

'Ah.'

Father Gunn turned with irritation as he once more switched his attention from the older girl back to her nervous younger sister.

The priest's irritated voice and the steely look of the eyes behind the silver-rimmed spectacles made Sapphire want to sink into the depths of the sofa.

Maybe that wasn't the best way to begin, Father Gunn admitted to himself. He regretted his tetchiness as he took in the wretched expression of the younger girl; but what *was* a good way to begin in a situation like this?

Sapphire wondered what he meant. Getting pregnant was terrible – but surely for her more than anyone. Everyone was upset, but it was *her* life that was messed up. What she'd done, she'd brought upon herself. With some help from Jay.

On the sofa beside her, Miranda tutted in annoyance and Sapphire knew, with a rush of gratitude, that her sister just had exactly the same thought.

'It's not a thing that usually happens in Hungry. Not to

our girls. We're not that kind of a place. You come from a good, caring family. I don't understand.'

Sapphire said nothing. How could he understand? What did Father Gunn know about the kind of boredom and yearning that made you want to tear up the whole world? How could a priest ever understand that?

'I'm sorry,' she whispered.

'Yes. Now what's to be done about it? Well, that's what I'm here to sort out,' the priest continued in a gentle tone, but he threw a tetchy glance at Miranda again and Sapphire knew her sister must be giving him one of her looks.

Ever since Miranda had started university, she and Dad had had endless rows about religion. They'd argue in slogans and soundbites that each of them had specially rehearsed prior to Miranda's Sunday visit home. Thought control of the masses, Miranda would shout. The school of the soul, Dad would respond, though he never had time to go to church. Sapphire could never decide who was right so she'd just put on the TV and tune out.

'Isn't this something that Sapphire should decide for herself?' said Miranda.

The priest ignored that, though he was grateful that someone had at last said the girl's name. 'Now, Sapphire—' he began.

'Where's Mum?' Sapphire interrupted. 'Why isn't she here?'

'She's very busy,' her father answered, but he looked uncomfortable.

'And very upsetting this must be for her,' added the priest. 'This must have caused her a lot of pain.'

'Only till about eight p.m.,' said Miranda. 'Then the gin kicks in.'

A fierce hush fell upon the room. Miranda fidgeted with

her hair and looked ashamed. Sapphire knew all about her sister's frustration with a mother who shut herself out of the world and inside a cupboard most nights. Some years ago, Miranda had looked at that closed door and yelled that she would never let *her* life come to a dead end like that.

'I'm glad to hear that,' Jude had shouted back, from behind the door.

'Mum should be here,' Sapphire burst out. She couldn't breathe. There was no air in the cramped and stifling living room. She turned to her dad. 'I want Mum.'

Did her mother know Father Gunn was here? Sapphire wondered. Surely she wouldn't have agreed to Father Gunn coming round when she meant Sapphire to get rid of the baby. This must be Dad's plan to put a stop to that, to corner her into keeping it. Mum wouldn't abandon her like this, if she knew. Would she?

'I want Mum,' Sapphire repeated.

'Now, now,' said Father Gunn uncomfortably.

He leaned over and patted Sapphire's hand kindly but still with that stern expression in his eyes, as if he didn't know which treatment, tender or harsh, she deserved.

Boris looked out of the window. The heat was blasting though it wasn't yet lunchtime. Outside, trees and blue sky shimmered as if made of molten glass.

'She wants Mum,' said Miranda, angrily.

'The church is here to help and support young girls like you, Sapphire,' said Father Gunn in the soothing tone that he used for the old and dying. 'We have a special fund to help you with any expenses like prams and cots and clothes – not always brand new, of course, but good enough. We often find that with the right support, many of our girls get on nicely. Some even get back to their studies when the little one starts school.'

'This isn't her only option,' said Miranda, her aggression building.

'Miranda,' warned Dad.

'I want Mum,' said Sapphire yet again, but no one seemed to hear. Her voice had shrunk to a babyish whimper.

'We don't want Sapphire to do something that she might regret for the rest of her life – and beyond,' said Father Gunn ominously. 'Something that might scar her emotionally for the rest of her life, something she and the rest of the family couldn't live with. You don't want to tear your family apart, Sapphire.'

Sapphire tried to catch her dad's eyes but he was steadfastly avoiding hers. She wanted to run out of the room but was unable to move.

'I don't want to!' she burst out. 'I don't want to – to – don't want any of this – I'm not having a baby. I'm not selling it. I'm not doing anything. I'm *not* having it – I can't do that, I can't. Mum said I don't have to – she said I'm too young.'

Everyone stared out of the window. The heat poured in through the glass.

Father Gunn mopped his brow and wished he was elsewhere. He looked beyond the grounds of Hunger Home to the streets that radiated around the hill and imagined himself sipping a cool drink in the shady porch of a villa, being fussed over by one of the officious, fund-raising women that Hungry seemed to breed.

Though on recent parish visits he had been dragged into all kinds of petty disagreements – such as who was sneaking out in the dead of night to break the heatwave ban on garden hoses. They all were, Father Gunn had decided, as he walked past flowerbeds that were suspiciously lush after two months of drought.

At the best of times, the inhabitants of the Drives felt their squat bungalows, inaptly named after the highlands of the world, were far grander than they actually were, while those in the Avenues thought their villas indisputably worthy of the regal figures they took their names from. Those in Oak Gardens, Chestnut Grove and Birch Crescent told themselves their woodland names lent a countrified air to their patch of Hungry, even though the trees had long been toppled in favour of manicured hedges and dwarf conifers. All sorts of jealousies and resentments festered in those neat streets, and the long weeks of the heatwave, Father Gunn reflected, had brought out the worst in people.

So his heart had lifted at the thought of coming up to Hunger Home today and doing something of real importance.

But it wasn't working out as he'd thought.

'Well now,' Father Gunn's voice slipped into the awkward silence that had fallen upon the room. He took a moment to refocus and remind himself of his task. 'Well, you're upset,' he soothed. 'Of course. Scared too. It's something you might have thought about before. It's certainly going to be hard all round. This is not something that should happen to a girl of fourteen. But we have some very good people,' he was talking to Dad now, 'who can help with all this . . .' the priest's eyes scanned the room, searching for a word, 'this upset. Let me send someone.'

He turned back to Sapphire, and stopped for a second, confused. She really didn't look like the kind of a girl who would get into trouble like this. Pretty, polite, just a regular young girl. But what did he know about young girls? Look at the way they dressed (he inadvertently slipped a glance at Miranda's tight jeans and reflected that, having set his heart at twelve years old on being a priest, he'd been spared all dealings with a young madam like that).

'Let me send over someone,' he repeated, 'to help you through this difficult time.' The priest paused for a moment to let his memory catch up, and ended on a jubilant note as the right name popped to mind, 'Sapphire.'

Sapphire half-believed him. He sounded as if he really did want to help but the stern, occasionally distant look weakened her trust. And the help that he offered wasn't what she wanted. She wanted to jump right out of this nightmare.

'There's a boy involved too,' Miranda reminded everyone. 'You can't just blame Sapphire.'

Now Father Gunn's eyes settled upon Miranda, weighing her up, gauging her words, seeming to decide that she was the kind of girl who didn't get herself pregnant, because she was clever enough not to. And perhaps that was worse, his eyes seemed to suggest.

Miranda knew that was not worse. She didn't even know if that was really what the priest was thinking yet a flash of anger spread across her skin, burning her neck and face red.

'The boy is another matter,' said Father Gunn, noting the flush. 'Do we know who he is?'

Sapphire looked at a coffee stain on the carpet.

'We haven't got to the root of that yet, Father,' said Boris. 'But I will.'

You won't, thought Sapphire.

'We don't only blame Sapphire,' Boris told Miranda. 'I haven't forgotten there's a boy involved, but your sister should have known better, even if he didn't. We've brought you both up to know how to behave.'

The anger her father injected into the word *boy* made Sapphire's skin crawl.

'You and Mum have never given us the slightest hint of how to behave sexually,' said Miranda. 'We've had to figure it all out ourselves. And Sapphire figured it wrong.'

Flicking a strand of hair from her cheek, she leaned over the table and pretended to linger over a choice of biscuit from the selection Dad had put out for Father Gunn, but her lingering was really to make sure that the priest would have plenty of opportunity to spot, in the gape of skin between her short top and her jeans, the two-week-old tattoo of a wicked little red snake near the base of her spine, just above the line of her pants. She'd christened it Emily after the inspirational Emilys in history, she said, though Sappire couldn't even think of one.

At long last, Miranda picked the only chocolate biscuit on the plate, the one Dad must have placed on top to draw attention away from the pile of cheap crumble creams underneath, and placed it between her teeth – though she would never actually bite or swallow it. The thing was loaded with sugar and fat. But, satisfied that she had flaunted her self-determination to Father Gunn, and shown him that she was absolutely her own woman, *not* the kind of girl who would let anyone else determine her fate, now that she was sure everyone in the room understood that, Miranda found herself at a loss as to what else to do or say.

So Miranda did something that she had taught herself to do well in a difficult situation: she stood up and strutted, with an air of absolute defiance, to the door.

It was only once she was on the other side of the

door with the biscuit in her hand, licking the slime of chocolate from her lips, that Miranda remembered that none of this was about her. It was about Sapphire. But now it was too late to do anything more to help her sister. She'd done all she could. She couldn't turn back now and spoil her exit. Sapphire was on her own. She had tried to help and now it was up to her little sister to save herself.

On the roof of the tower, once the priest had gone, Sapphire took out the mobile phone she'd nabbed from Miranda's rucksack in the hall and tapped out Emma's mobile number. Jude was calling and calling her name. It echoed all through the rooms of their living quarters.

Well, let her call. She should have been there.

No matter what crisis there was, no matter if the entire population of Hunger Home was at death's door, all at once, her mother should have been there. She should never have left her to face Father Gunn like that.

'Sapphire! Are you up there?' Jude's voice floated up from the bedroom window below. 'Come down. Please. I didn't know about Father Gunn. Your dad brought him here behind my back.'

Sapphire stayed silent. She heard Boris's irate voice. She couldn't hear exactly what he said but she could guess.

'Hi!' Emma's voice called from the phone. She sounded so normal and happy.

'Emmy, I'm up on top of the tower,' said Sapphire. 'Something – something really bad's happened. Can you come over? Right now?'

'What's going on? Hey, have you finally got yourself a mobile?'

'No, it's Miranda's.'

Sapphire was the only teenager in Hungry, she had

complained many times, who didn't have her own mobile. Dad just shrugged. He couldn't afford one for himself, he said, never mind one for Sapphire, on which she would no doubt run up enormous bills.

'Emmy, come right now,' said Sapphire. 'Meet me up on the tower – but don't come to the front door, don't let anybody see you. Use the back fire stairs.'

'OK. Five mins. See you,' said Emma, breathless with curiosity.

Sapphire let out a great sigh. Emma would help her. She should have talked to her before.

Since nursery school, Emma's life and her own had been intertwined. Together, they'd learned to roller skate and cycle and swim, to braid and bead their hair; together, they'd taken up and outgrown dancing classes, gymnastics, sleepovers, books and boy bands and building dens among Hunger Home's vast grounds. Games of Truth or Dare revealed their deepest selves. Crazes flared and died between them as they searched through magazines, mapping the clues and rules of girldom, seeking out the heart and soul of the world from the realm of their bedrooms.

Together this last year, they'd spent their spare time practising signatures on the backs of magazines and kissing skills on the backs of their hands. They'd customized their jeans and shoes, swapped make-up, scrutinizing every detail of their skin, hair and body, remodelling what they were and learning what they could be. In the process, they'd sealed a glossy new veneer over their scruffy girlhood. And all the time they'd talked, about everything there was to talk about in the world, but most of all about boys.

In late spring, it all gelled. As the dark nights lightened

and the rainy west wind that blew in from the sea lessened, the young people of Hungry began to spill out on to the streets. The two girls looked at each other and saw that it was time for them to be out there too, showing off their thrilling, potent new selves.

'We did it,' smirked Emma, as they walked around Hungry, unable to take their eyes off their changed reflections in the windows of parked cars. 'Now we look real. We're what we used to look at and wish we were. Now *we're* chocolate.'

And it seemed she was right. Boys stopped in the street to talk to them. Men slowed down in cars to look and whistle and call.

'Who'd have thought?' Emma giggled. 'You and me – last summer we were scruffy nobodies.'

And now they were chocolate girls. On the outside, anyway. But inside? Sapphire had learned the tricks to make herself look like one, but beneath the veneer of make-up and clothes, poses and attitude, she felt more unsure, awkward and self-conscious than she'd ever been. Somehow, she couldn't find the words to tell Emma. She had a horrible sense that even Emma wouldn't understand.

Sapphire kept expecting that her smooth chocolate veneer would crack and everyone would see that underneath she was really as ordinary as mud. So when the gorgeous Jay Webb fell for her, she couldn't believe it.

Grace noticed their transformations right away and brought them into her gang. That was Grace's way. She contained the competition. You were either out or in; there was no in-between. Last summer they were too little-girlish, left on the sidelines. This summer they had earned their place in the heart of the gang.

But it was such hard work. Far harder than school.

Grace set the rules.

Rule number one: never look less than gorgeous, which meant continually applying fresh make-up and washing hair every second day. Rule two: no jeans at weekends. On weekends, you had to pull out all the stops – best clothes, best hair and make-up. Rule three: never wear the same outfit two days in a row – which often reduced Sapphire and Emma to swapping tops and belts in desperation, as neither had Grace's vast wardrobe.

Pierced navels were cool, pierced noses not. Fake tattoos, body glitter, ankle chains and baggy T-shirts were too gross to be allowed. Flirting was a priority, the conquest of boys the ultimate goal. Except for one thing – and about that Grace was ruthless.

You could do whatever it took to get the boy you wanted, except full sex. Only desperate, non-chocolate girls needed to do that, Grace implied. Not us. To do that meant a loss of power.

All you had to do, said Grace, was keep pretending you might.

Sapphire had ventured to disagree. At least, her body had. Secretly, subversively, it had disobeyed the most crucial rule of Grace's gang.

But Grace, it seemed, was right. Sapphire had slept with Jay, and now she had lost her power over him. She'd lost him to the power of Grace.

Emma ran out of the trees and raced across the grass towards the rear of Hunger Home. Her feet clanged on the metal fire stairs that zigzagged up the back of the mansion.

Minutes later, when Emma flopped down beside her, breathless and groaning with the heat, Sapphire could have cried with relief. Emma's fine blonde hair stuck sweatily to her forehead. She raked it back and laughed.

'If Grace could see me now I'd be for it!' She frowned at Sapphire. 'If she could see *you* now . . . what's with the baggy T-shirt and jeans – Sapphy, it's Saturday! You must be melting in all that. Are you ill? What's up?'

'No – not exactly,' said Sapphire.

'Well, what is it?' Emma sat back against the low wall of the tower. 'What's happened? You chuck Jay and—'

'I didn't chuck him.'

Sapphire turned her face away from Emma. Swallowed. Took a breath.

'Emmy, I'm pregnant.'

Emma let out a laugh. Stared at Sapphire. Then slapped her, hard, on the arm.

'Stop it.'

'I am.'

Emma stared some more then stood up.

'You are joking.'

'No.'

'But you can't be,' Emma said in a small, strained voice. 'You wouldn't – you *can't* be.'

'I'm sorry,' said Sapphire.

All she seemed to do was apologize to everyone about it. She didn't know what else to do.

'How could you be?'

'That safe time, Emmy – we got it wrong,' began Sapphire.

Emma looked really scared. She cut in. 'We?'

'Remember you said . . . I mean, it's not your fault or anything.'

'Whatever I said's got nothing to do with it,' said Emma.

Sapphire swallowed. What was happening? She knew Emma would be shocked but she had imagined them huddled together up here on the tower, crying a bit, then talking it all through as they always did whenever one of them had a problem. She'd never expected Emma to react like this.

A long silence fell between them. The sun sent down a furnace blast of heat. A lorry groaned, straining round the circular streets.

'What's it like?' said Emma at last. She had turned her back on Sapphire to look out over Hungry.

'What?'

'You know.'

Sapphire stared at the back of Emma's head. What could she say? That at first it had been embarrassing and awkward. It felt like a ridiculous thing to do. But then she began to feel she was unravelling at the edges, thread by thread. As if she was no longer made up of bones and muscle and skin but had become molten sensation. It was a vast feeling. And amid all that was the strangeness of someone else's touch on skin that no one else had touched since she was tiny.

'It was nice,' said Sapphire.

Emma turned round. 'Really? Not, you know, yuk.'

'No,' said Sapphire.

Emma sighed and pulled at the frayed edge of her denim shorts.

'Why are you so angry?' murmured Sapphire.

Emma said nothing, avoiding her eyes.

'Emmy?'

'Because you've spoilt everything!' Emma burst out. 'We've had a great summer, the best ever, and you've ruined it.' Her cute rabbit face crumpled. 'How can we be best friends now?'

'Emmy—'

'Well, how can we? Me at school and you someone's

mummy. How can we?' Emma looked panic-stricken. 'It's impossible.'

Sapphire couldn't breathe. This was worse than Mum and Dad, worse than Father Gunn, worse than anything. She had expected their reactions, but not this, not from Emma.

She couldn't lose Emma. She couldn't bear that.

'But I won't have it,' said Sapphire. 'Mum says I don't have to.'

She'd wanted to tell Emma all about her conversations with Miranda, about the TV couple who wanted to buy the baby, about Father Gunn and Dad cornering her behind Mum's back – about everything that had been happening.

'You'll have an – an abortion?' Emma drew back. 'Sapphy, that's so gross.'

She sounded like Grace. That was Grace's cutting tone of voice. The disgusted pout of her lips was a straight copy of Grace too.

'I have to,' said Sapphire. 'Then everything'll get back to normal.'

'No it won't. Not now you've told me. Why'd you have to tell me?'

'We – we always tell each other everything.'

'Well, I wish you'd never told me that. And you're lying. You haven't been telling me everything.' Betrayal was pink and bitter on Emma's face. 'Have you? You never told me you and Jay were sleeping together. Why didn't you tell me that?'

Sapphire lowered her eyes. Why hadn't she? Because it was between her and Jay. And because she couldn't. It was against the rule of Grace. The opposite of what a chocolate girl was supposed to be.

'Sleeping with him's one thing.' Emma stood up. 'But getting pregnant, having an abortion – that's not us. That's totally yuk.'

She began to walk away towards the fire stairs, then stopped. 'I've looked it up in Mum's medical books and it's horrible. They burn them, you know. The babies. They'll yank it out of you with a hook and they'll burn it up. We can't be friends if you do that. Every time I look at you, I'll think of it.'

'I won't do that then.' Sapphire felt desperate. 'I'll – I'll just have it adopted.'

'But then you'll have to be pregnant. You'll be pregnant for months.' Emma's eyes dropped to the ground. 'It'll be so embarrassing,' she muttered. 'Everyone'll be talking about you and they'll think that I – that *I'm* . . .'

She tailed off but Sapphire knew what it was that Emma couldn't say. People would think that Emma was like her because they were best friends. If Emma stood by her, it would be at a huge cost to herself. She'd never be allowed to stay in Grace's gang, for a start. Boys would look at her differently if she stuck by a pregnant loser. She'd be risking everything that she'd become.

'Bye,' she told Emma.

'Sapphy, I'm sorry, I—'

'Just go.'

Sapphire turned away.

She listened to the clang of Emma's feet on the metal stairs of the fire escape.

Then she remembered something, and rushed across to the top of the stairs.

'Emma? Don't tell Jay!' Emma didn't stop. 'Don't, Emma. Please. Don't tell anyone. Not Grace or your mum. No one!'

But Emma kept running down the fire escape until Sapphire couldn't see her. All that was left was the echo of her footsteps. And then she was gone.

Sapphire stayed up on the tower. She hadn't eaten all day, but couldn't face human contact. So she sat looking out over the rooftops of Hungry to the skyscrapers and slate roofs, the chimneys and steeples, bridges and flyovers of the city. She looked past the silver snake of the river, beyond the glint of a distant plane to the gleaming line of the sea.

As little girls, she and Emma had decided that the noisy boiler in the basement of Hunger Home was probably a dragon. They'd planned how to befriend the dragon – by feeding it lots of gingersnap biscuits – a dragon's favourite treat, said Emma, who knew her fairy tales. Once sweetened up, they'd persuade the dragon to fly them over Hungry, out beyond the city, beyond the sea.

Up here on the tower, last spring, they'd flicked through *The Teen Guide to Life: Peer Pressure, Exams, Sex, Addiction, Loss, Depression and Family Problems.* They forgot suicide, said Emma, adding that you'd want to end it all if you read that lot. They forgot boredom too, Sapphire said. They'd chucked the book off the tower and watched it plummet to the ground, its pages fluttering like a weighty-winged bird.

They were stuck here at fourtedium, then there was fiftedium and sixtedium to get through, they joked, until the in-between years of teen boredom would end. Then, they said, their real lives would begin.

Oh, Emmy.

Sapphire lay down on the floor of the tower roof and curled up into a ball. With Jay, she'd seemed to zip through all that tedium. She'd thought her real life was beginning, earlier than expected. She never imagined it could end up like this.

And never thought she could lose Emma. She remembered the look on her friend's face.

Sapphire understood. Right before Emma's eyes, she had changed from soulmate into something completely alien. Somebody who was stupid enough to get pregnant. Somebody who was going to end up a teenage single mother or a girl who'd given her baby away or who'd had an abortion. It was all so far removed from everything they'd thought they were or wanted to be. She had betrayed Emma.

Sapphire lay curled up on the ground for a long time. The sun burned through her clothes. She'd been evicted from her own life and it was all her own doing.

What if Emma told Jay? Or Grace? Or her mother? Or all of them? Then it would be all over Hungry. Everyone would know. For the first time in her life Sapphire couldn't trust her best friend.

She picked up the phone that she'd left on the ground and made her mind go blank. If she thought about what she was going to do then she'd never do it.

She tapped out Jay's mobile number. She had no idea what words might spill out of her mouth, if any would, when he answered.

The phone rang and rang. Her scalp prickled with fear as all of a sudden he was there. But it was only his voice. His answering-machine message. Sapphire let out a breath of relief. Then looked over the trees and roofs of Hungry to Grace's large villa. Jay always had his phone with him. He always answered, even at the dinner table, despite his parents' complaints; even in the middle of classes in school. He'd had his phone confiscated umpteen times for that.

What was stopping him answering now, in the middle of the holidays?

He must be busy with *her.* Sapphire imagined him entangled with Grace in her bedroom or in the exotic oriental summer house, which Grace called a pagoda, at the bottom of her garden.

He had no right to be free, doing whatever he liked. This was his baby too. He'd taken exactly the same risks as she had and yet it was only her life that was ruined. His life was still all his own. He knew nothing of any of this. It wasn't fair.

Sapphire picked up the phone again, thought a moment, then punched in a text message. Well, he'd know now. And that would spoil things with Grace.

The second before she sent it, Sapphire deleted every word.

She switched off the phone and stuffed it in her jeans' pocket. The sun was still high in the sky, but it would fall. And she could go down into the grounds and wait until it did, until the dusk.

She clanged down the fire stairs, not caring if anyone heard. She wouldn't stop for anything. Even if Dad came out and tried to haul her back indoors she'd scream and kick and fight until she was free.

Sapphire made it clear of the house and ran hard for the trees.

What clues, thought Sapphire, as she hid in the thick of the trees near the entrance gate and waited for dusk to fall, what clues had any of the adults, the gatekeepers to the world, ever given her about anything that mattered?

'Be good,' they'd say. 'If you can't be good, be careful.'

And that was about it. Jeanne Moreau was the only adult

who had ever given her any clues that meant anything. And what did she say?

That life was about risk, about now, no time for nostalgia; you had to keep going, there were things you had to live through, all sorts of experiences and feelings that you couldn't put into words and it was those indescribable, intangible things that would sear you and brand you and make you the person you had to be.

After it is gone . . .

But would anything or anyone that mattered to you ever really be gone? Wouldn't something linger within you, colouring the rest of your life and what you were, even if you didn't want it to?

Like Emma, like Jay, like the tiny bean of life inside her.

How come it took Jeanne Moreau, a photo on a wall, to tell her that? And what did Mum and Dad expect when she'd been surrounded by all those Moreaus since she was born? Was it really such a shock that she'd chosen risk when the Moreau in the hallway had reminded her that *'life is risking'* every time she stepped out of the door into the world, every day of her life?

At dusk, she heard the sirens. Then, after an agony of waiting, the crash into the undergrowth that she'd been hoping for. She pushed through the bushes and branches towards the place of the crash.

He was slumped against the wall, next to the chestnut trees, panting.

When he saw her, he sat bolt upright, soaked in sweat.

'It's only me,' whispered Sapphire and he relaxed.

Then leaned forward, tense again, when she told him what she wanted.

'Why?' he asked.

Sapphire hesitated. She didn't know why. The impulse had burst upon her during the long wait for him in the trees. She leaned forward too.

'I feel so bad I want to die,' she confessed. 'But I don't know how to die. I don't know how I'd do it.'

Up on the tower she had tried to imagine the ways – hurling herself off the tower, razoring her wrist, swallowing handfuls of pills, holding her head under bathwater, standing in the path of a speeding car. Jumping into a river or reservoir wasn't an option. The water levels were too low. But she knew she'd never do any of them. They were all too painful, violent or uncertain in outcome.

She didn't want to hurt herself. She was frightened of pain and blood. She just wanted to escape the mess she was in, have her life back and feel safe again in her own skin.

'So I need to do something,' she explained to the boy, 'and I thought of you.'

The outside world had gone quiet, now the sirens had stopped.

'Me?' he said.

His eyes were as deep and still as the dusk shadows around them.

'Please,' said Sapphire.

Gilbert only looked at her. He had such a confusion of feeling he didn't know what else to do.

'Can – can you run?' he finally asked.

She smiled. 'I can run.'

He smiled back, nervously. The scent of smoke was all about him. She breathed it in and a delicate fire spread under her skin.

'I know a house out on the edges of Hungry,' she said. 'It's got a pagoda in the garden.'

'What's that?' He looked down, embarrassed that he didn't know. Then laughed at himself.

'It's an oriental garden room.' Sapphire laughed too. 'A kind of summer house with a stupid name.'

Gilbert nodded, eyes shining as he recognized the description. He had seen it, had thought about it as a target, but hadn't known that's what it was called.

'It's made of wood,' said Sapphire.

He knew. His brow wrinkled in thought.

'Can you remember the exact garden?'

'Oh, yes,' said Sapphire.

Gilbert got up and walked over to a huge beech tree with a deep nook in its thick trunk, reached in and took out a black plastic bin bag. He rummaged inside and brought out a can of petrol. It glugged as he set it down on the ground beside her.

Sapphire's heartbeat quickened. Could she really do this? Would she? Unsure and trembly, she picked up the can. It gave another thick glug. She liked the sound.

She looked at the boy.

'What's your name?' she asked.

She'd seen him at school, she was sure. He was a year or two older so it was strange she didn't know his name because she was well aware of who most of the older boys were. What had made her overlook him? He had a gaze you could fall into if you looked long enough. But there was a stillness there so deep and intense that most people would look away. And that stillness was part of what made him unnoticeable, she guessed. He wouldn't be part of the crowd; he'd be out on the edges, someone in the background who never came within her line of vision because she had been focused on those at the centre of things.

Gilbert knew that too. He didn't stop to think about

whether he trusted her or not, about whether it was a good idea to get any closer to this girl, who knew his dangerous secret. Sapphire Dean had rooted so instantly and deeply in his imagination that he felt as if he knew her, even though he didn't.

'Gilbert Lemon,' he said.

Gilbert, thought Sapphire, what a name.

She wrapped the can of petrol back in the bin bag and snuggled it under her arm.

'Let's go then, Gil,' she said.

The pagoda was in the garden of the large, fat, white villa that was Grace's home. The pagoda was the place where Grace held court, deciding who was and who wasn't a chocolate girl, who was allowed in her special gang – outsiders were ignored, shunned, ridiculed or bullied, depending on Grace's whim. From the pagoda, she set the rules because she was the most chocolate of them all.

She had the longest, sleekest hair; the leanest legs, the brownest tummy; the most perfect teeth and skin. A Spanish grandmother had given her looks and mannerisms a touch of exoticism that out-magicked the charms of the rest of the girls in Hungry, no matter how pretty they were. She captivated everyone – boys, girls, shopkeepers and teachers. She could swear under her breath at someone's mother or steal lipgloss testers from the chemist, and get away with it. Grace helped herself to whatever she wanted in life because she could. She stole from her father's wallet, her mother's wardrobe, plundered local shops for style magazines and make-up, and took whoever's boyfriend she wanted.

All the other girls laboured to become more Grace-like. They grew their hair and combed it sleek with wax. They went on starvation diets and applied fake tan to mimic her lean brown legs and stomach. They spent ages in front of their mirrors practising her serene smile with its edge of sultriness.

But the leaner, sleeker and more prettied-up everyone else got, the more Grace would distil herself into something even more exotic. If the others cropped their denims shorter, she'd retaliate by wearing hers slung extra low. She became as thin as a crisp, grew her hair down past her waist, and tanned herself deeper still. There was no out-Gracing Grace.

There was only this, decided Sapphire.

She glugged the petrol from the can, all around the edges of the pagoda, wetting the base wood, as Gilbert Lemon told her to. Then she trickled it in a line all the way up to the wall at the back where he waited. When she reached him, he took a white pebble from his jeans pocket and placed it where the trickle ended in the grass.

The moon had climbed high in the near-dark sky. Its light glistened upon his skin. A liquid sensation ran through Sapphire, from her scalp down to her toes, as she watched his hands twist a bit of newspaper into a long taper.

'Now light it.'

He held out the unlit taper and she took it. He lit a match and set the taper alight. A film of perspiration glued her clothes to her skin. Sapphire tried to hand it back.

'You do it.'

But he wouldn't.

'Do it and you won't want to die,' he urged.

So she touched the line of petrol with the burning taper.

'Drop it!' he ordered, the instant it caught. 'Run!'

She was running except she couldn't feel herself move. It was as if she'd left her body behind.

'Now watch,' said Gilbert, once they'd reached the end of the garden and clambered over the wall.

Sapphire looked back over the wall and let out a cry. The pagoda was a living sculpture of flame.

There was a scream from inside the house and a small dog's high, vicious bark. Light spilled out across the garden.

'Down!' Gilbert pulled her to the ground. 'Follow me.'

'Just a second,' said Sapphire. She couldn't resist one last look.

Grace's mother had run down into the garden, screaming. Grace's father followed, yelling into his mobile phone.

'They're on their way, angel,' he shouted, stuffing his phone into his pocket and hurried to support Grace's mother with his arm as if he thought she might fall down. 'Be here in minutes.'

'Too late, it's too late,' sobbed the woman. 'My beautiful pagoda.'

'I'll get you another,' soothed her husband. 'We'll alarm the whole garden. This will never happen again. And I'll use every contact I have,' suddenly he was furious, 'to catch the monster who's done this.'

And then Sapphire saw Grace. She was standing on the lawn, watching the blaze of the pagoda. But the distress that Sapphire wanted to see on the other girl's face wasn't there. The light of the fire showed that clearly.

Grace was almost smiling. She stood just behind her parents and as her eyes slid from the burning pagoda to her sobbing mother, the look on her face was concealed delight.

'Sapphire! We've got to move now!'

Gilbert pulled Sapphire sharply by the arm and she had to snap out of her amazement and follow.

In houses all around them, lights snapped on, doors flung open, shouts and barks filled the air. They raced through a neighbouring villa's garden, ignoring the pandemonium. The chaos gave them time to make it to a high-banked, almost dried-up stream. Here, they jumped down and began to stumble over rocks and stones, following the track of the stream, a long silver moon path scattered with shadows.

They reached an arch of darkness. A stone bridge.

Gilbert pulled Sapphire underneath. Sirens blared close by.

'We're safe here. All we have to do now,' Gilbert whispered, breathing heavily, 'is get across the road and jump the wall into the trees. Then we're home.'

'That's the road?' said Sapphire. She couldn't see how they could have got to the road so quickly. Then she understood. Gilbert had mapped Hungry in a different way from anyone else. He knew it by the path of the stream that wound through many of the back gardens of the houses and fed into the Hunger, a western artery of the much larger river that ran through the city and into the sea. He never used the roads and streets. That's how he'd never got caught.

They climbed up the steep, dry bank of the stream. It crumbled away under hand and foot and they struggled to make it up to the top. Once there, all they had to do was push through the hedge and they were on the pavement, directly across the road from Hunger Home. It should now be too dark for the watchers on the hill to see them.

'Brilliant,' said Sapphire.

They were about to run when Gilbert pulled her down on to the crumbling bank of ground so hard that her face hit the dirt. Sapphire raised her head and saw the slow, almost noiseless crawl of a police car on the road.

They waited. Once they were sure the road was safe, they pushed through the hedge, on to the pavement, scanned the scene for people, then ran.

When they reached the other side of the road, Gilbert swerved to avoid something. And stumbled, in the worst place of all, just within the orange glow of the street lamp by the bus shelter.

Sapphire grabbed his arm to stop him sprawling on the pavement. Cursing, he found his feet.

Someone drew back into the shadows.

Sapphire stared in fright. Who was it?

'Come *on*,' urged Gil.

The slow purr of a car came from further up the road. Gilbert grabbed Sapphire's hand. Then, as the long reach of the car's headlamps hit the back of their heads and lit upon the face of the person in the bus shelter, he stalled too.

He looked at the woman and she looked back.

The police car revved and sped towards them.

'Gil!'

Sapphire yanked his hand to break his trance and ran.

Gil unlocked himself from the woman's eyes and moved.

They scrambled over the wall of Hunger Home and fell into nettles. They raced across the dark lawns to the sanctuary of the trees and the thick rhododendron bushes on the far side of the grounds. They hid there until the police invaded the grounds with torches.

'The tower,' said Sapphire. It was the only place she could think of.

Keeping to the shadows, they raced to the back of the Home and crept as noiselessly as they could up the metal stairs of the fire escape, to the flat roof of the tower. They heard the police crunch across the gravel path, up to the door of the Home. They waited, huddled together, hearts pounding, but no one came.

'I like it here,' Gilbert said. They lay flat on their backs on the cool stone of the tower roof, floppy with relief now the police were gone. 'You're outside the world. Almost part of the sky. I don't like the world.'

'Neither do I,' said Sapphire. 'I used to. Not now.'

'What changed?' asked Gilbert.

'Me,' she said and turned her head to look at him, instead of the stars. 'Why don't you like the world, Gil?'

He liked the way she called him Gil. No one had ever called him that. It felt right. Now he would be Gil.

'Why fire? How did it start?' she said.

He couldn't find the words to answer her, couldn't explain anything. All he knew was that when dusk made everything a shadow of its daylight self and he had fire in his hands, then he felt right.

'What if it got out of control and someone got burned? Or killed?' The question had begun to trouble Sapphire, now that her excitement had cooled.

Gil shook his head. 'I'm too careful. I control it. I watch a place and check it out to make sure nobody's going to get hurt.'

He knew that wasn't wholly true. Lately, he had depended more and more on the fire crews getting there fast. But their increasing speed meant he was more at risk than ever. Months of harsh sun had burned Hungry as dry as tinder and this made Gil's mastery of fire less certain, much more down to chance than he would admit.

'You didn't tonight. We just went for it.'

She was right, Gil knew. Tonight, he had been far more focused on Sapphire's presence than on the fire. Whether anyone got hurt was the last thing on his mind. His concentration had been scattered. That was why, in the street, he didn't see the woman until it was too late, and almost fell.

Sapphire was remembering the woman too, remembering how Gil had stared at her.

'Do you know her – that Mad Hatter woman? She's a cleaner at the Home.'

Gil fidgeted with the matchbox in his jeans' pocket, rattling the matches inside. He didn't want to think about the woman now. He wanted to make Sapphire focus on *him*. There was only one way.

He sat up.

'Want to do the fire of all fires?' he said.

She sat up too, all attention now. So close he could feel her breath on his face.

'Where?'

'Near where I live.'

'Where do you live?' asked Sapphire. She hadn't given it a thought.

'Out on the edge,' laughed Gil, because he did.

Sapphire laughed too. 'I believe that. But what's the fire of all fires?' She leaned even closer. Her long hair touched his arm.

'Tell me.'

'Well, we could muck about, burning up sheds and tabogas forever but—'

'Pagodas.'

Sapphire laughed again and he smiled back, unembarrassed now because whatever she thought of him, she knew he wasn't stupid.

'Right. But there's bigger things than that.'

Her eyes shone and the thrill of excitement on her mouth turned his heart over.

'Why's a girl like you doing this?' he suddenly asked. 'What's wrong in your life?'

She fidgeted, looked down, pulled up a strand of grass.

'You know.'

He didn't but he left it alone. He could hear in her voice that she didn't want to explain.

She stood up. 'I want to see this place where we could do the fire of all fires.'

A howl came from the house below them.

'What do they do that for? It gives me the creeps.' Gil laughed softly.

'Wouldn't you howl if you were stuck in there day after day? In summer they usually get out in the grounds for walks or for afternoon tea, but it's been too hot. They're going stir crazy.' She sighed, thinking of her own imprisonment. 'It's late. I should go. I'm in too much trouble already.'

Gil looked at her and wondered what she'd done. Covered in moonlight, she looked too lovely to be in trouble.

'Tomorrow night,' he urged.

Sapphire turned back to him and smiled.

They stood up, too close to be comfortable, but neither moving apart. Sapphire recognized the tension in the moment.

It was the moment you might kiss. Especially after what they'd just done. There was only a hand span of distance between them.

But though they didn't move apart, neither did they close the distance between them. They didn't do anything at all, until Sapphire all of a sudden whirled around and disappeared down the metal fire escape. Leaving Gil on the tower alone, with the sound of her steps ringing in his head.

In the bathroom mirror, she was a girl made of silver.

Moonlight poured in through the window, drenching her in cool, invigorating light, landing like a slab of white mint on the bathroom floor. It turned her long, brown hair to a veil of silver and her blue eyes to pearl.

Outside, the moon had shone on his skin, turning him silver too, picking out the soft blue ridges of veins on the backs of his hands, as he'd shown her how to trickle a steady line of petrol. She had followed the points of light in his eyes as he moved the lit match to the paper taper; his quick, light breathing had matched hers as the fire zipped along the path they had made for it; his body, like hers, was a tense tinderbox of energy.

She relived their terrifying, exhilarating run, their body heat turning to cool sweat as they lay crashed together on the top of the tower. When she turned to him she saw his cheek and neck dripped with moonlight.

Sapphire knew why they hadn't kissed. It was because her body wasn't wholly hers any more. She couldn't kill the thought that whatever sensations she had might be shared by that tiny stranger inside.

And that's how it had started last time, with a kiss. That's how she had ended up in this mess. She'd followed the flow of her body, did as it urged, ignoring the voice in the back of her mind that said *stop*.

Who are you? Sapphire asked her reflection in the bathroom mirror. *What have you become?*

Lost, said the silver girl.

Then find yourself, said a different voice. The deep, smoky voice that Sapphire had imagined for Jeanne Moreau.

Sapphire turned around to the photo on the bathroom door.

How? she asked.

Do whatever you must, said Jeanne Moreau. *Just don't stay lost.*

And then another voice; no, more an impulse than a voice.

But what about me?

It came from deep inside her, and she knew who it was.

I have to look after myself first, she told it, *because I'm already here. I'm me.*

But I'm here too, it responded. *And I'm me.*

'No,' Sapphire cried to the estranged silver girl in the mirror. 'No.'

His scent clung to her like incense. Smoke and petrol. It was part of her now, the scent of who she had become. The scent of risk. She would keep it on her. She would not wash.

Gil went to bed so late it was almost time to get up again. His father let him alone so that when he woke the sun was beating hard upon the thin walls of the caravan.

He lay in his narrow bed, reliving every moment of the previous night. Something had changed in the Sapphire who lived in his head. She felt shadowy, less real. Gil sat up in bed and knew what had happened. The moment she took the taper from his hand and set fire to the pagoda, the real Sapphire had overlapped the imagined one he kept like a living dream in the landscape of his mind. And then there had been that extraordinary moment on the tower. It had left him so high that he ran all the way home, feeling as if his feet had grown wings.

Usually, Gilbert was slow as a slug in the heat of the day, though he was fast as a bat by night. Today, Gil leaped out of bed and grinned, just because he was alive.

Later, he would think about the woman who lurked on the edge of his mind.

But not now.

'Why's everyone cross?' asked Gretel.

She stood in the middle of their bedroom with one leg in her pyjama trousers, scratching her head and looking extremely cross herself.

'It's not you they're cross with, it's me,' said Sapphire.

'What did you do?'

Sapphire looked away. 'I was silly. Careless.'

'How? What did you do?'

Sapphire shrugged. 'I didn't think.'

'I do that lots,' said Gretel, still scratching furiously. Sapphire suddenly realized that Gretel seemed to have been scratching continuously for several days.

She looked at her little sister's head warily.

'I think I've got *things* again,' said Gretel ominously. 'You know, nots.'

Sapphire groaned. 'Nits.'

Gretel nodded and sat down beside Sapphire on the bed.

'You'd better tell Mum,' said Sapphire, backing away.

'I have but she's forgot. She's all cross. You do it. I'll get the comb and stuff.'

'No, Gretel.'

'Yes! It's your fault Mum's cross,' her little sister reminded her.

Gretel went off to organize the head lice paraphernalia. She'd been through it several times before so she knew the routine. Once she got over her disgust, Sapphire found the rhythm of combing and picking through Gretel's hair quite soothing.

'It's a shame really,' said Gretel. 'Killing all those babies.'

Sapphire froze in mid-comb. 'What babies?'

'The baby nits. They might have had a nice life,' Gretel giggled, 'running all over my head, as if that was their big world. But *I* wouldn't like that, would I?'

Sapphire swallowed. 'No.'

'They're driving me to subtraction,' decided Gretel. 'So poor little babies, they just have to go.'

'Sapphire,' said Boris from the doorway. He spoke so softly and unexpectedly that Sapphire dropped the comb.

'Oh,' he said, 'not again, Gretel.'

'It's not my fault!' Gretel protested. 'Mum says they like clean hair. That's why they like mine lots.'

'Never mind,' soothed Dad. 'I'll take over here, Sapphire. Your mum wants to see you downstairs.'

Sapphire handed him the comb. 'She's crawling.'

'Lovely.' Boris laughed for the first time in days.

'Dad,' whispered Sapphire. His laugh, that small semblance of normality, choked her up with sudden tears.

He must have heard the tears in her voice. But awkwardly, as if he didn't know what to do, he turned to Gretel and began combing.

'Dad, I'm really sorry,' said Sapphire, wishing more than anything that they could be normal with each other once again, that he would stop being so strange and awkward and hug all her bad feelings away. She thought she understood something of what her pregnancy had done to him – he had lost his role as her great protector. Sapphire had always seemed the timid one compared to Miranda and Gretel, and Boris had always enjoyed making a show of seeing off the threats of the outside world – anything from big bad wolves to thunderstorms – that once scared her.

The one thing he hadn't reckoned that he would have to protect Sapphire from was herself.

Suddenly, he put his hand on her shoulder and when she looked at him she saw how upset he was.

'Go on downstairs,' he told her gently. Then, just as she relaxed a little, he frowned. 'Wait a minute. I haven't had a chance to ask you: where were you last night?' His frown deepened. 'Who were you with?'

'Just Emma.'

For the first time since he'd found out she was pregnant, her father looked her in the eye. 'I had the police at the door last night.'

Sapphire concentrated on keeping her face as expressionless as possible.

'The police?'

'They were searching the grounds for this fire-raiser – or fire-raisers. They'd seen a suspicious-looking couple and thought they were hiding out in the grounds. You don't know anything about this, Sapphire?'

'Me?' Sapphire feigned indignation. 'You think *I'm* a fire-raiser?'

Boris almost smiled. 'Well, no. But then I never thought,' the smile fell away, 'you'd end up like *this*, did I? You were with Emma?'

Sapphire nodded.

'Even though I asked you to stay in the house until—'

'Until when?' Sapphire burst out. 'You can't keep me

locked up in here forever, Dad. I can't bear it. I'm not a criminal!'

Boris sighed. 'Not forever, but for now. Does Emma know about all this?'

Sapphire knew what to say to that.

'No, definitely not.'

'Because this is family business. I don't want it round the whole of Hungry.'

'I know.'

'On you go then. Your mum wants to talk to you. And remember, I want you to stay in this house. For now.'

Sapphire walked downstairs, feeling dazed. One long day in the house had made her ready to tear walls down with boredom. Now she was to live indefinitely in a kind of girl-prison? What did 'for now' mean? How long was she to stay sealed off from the outside world? Until the baby was born? That was half a year away.

No, thought Sapphire.

Downstairs in the living room were Miranda, Mum and another woman who looked familiar, though Sapphire couldn't place her.

'Well, it's an option, perhaps,' Mum was saying hesitantly. 'It's certainly an option.'

The atmosphere of the room was so hot and tense that Sapphire wanted to walk right out again. She looked over at the window, open as far as its safety catch would let it, which was only a hand's span. Not a breath of air stirred the room.

'This is Angie Vaze,' said Miranda. She smiled in a rather awestruck way at the woman. Now Sapphire recognized her: it was the television news presenter who had been in Di Maggio's the other night.

'I can imagine how difficult this is for everyone,' said

Angie Vaze. Her voice had the tone of a newsreader breaking a dramatic news story: deliberately steady with the faint hint of a thrill. 'Heaven knows I don't want to add to that. But maybe this is the solution that will cause the least pain all round. Certainly,' a tentative little smile twitched at the corners of her mouth, 'it would make me the happiest woman in the world.'

She expected to get what she wanted, Sapphire saw. She had the air of someone who was used to getting what she wanted. And the practised way she modulated her voice and measured her smile put Sapphire on her guard. She tensed, remembering the ten-thousand-pound offer Miranda had told her about.

'Sapphire,' Angie Vaze smiled gently, 'I know your sister mentioned my idea to you. Maybe it surprised you but let me explain it all myself. You've found yourself in the most impossible situation. You're just a girl, far too young to take on the responsibility of a baby. And . . .' Angie Vaze bit her lip, 'well, it seems I'm too old to conceive one.'

She didn't look too old. The woman seemed to read Sapphire's thoughts.

'It's true. I've left it too late. I think I must have tried every known fertility treatment over the last few years and I'm at the end of the line.' Angie Vaze cleared her throat and swallowed. 'I long for a baby, Sapphire. And you're going to have one. But you really don't want to have it, do you?'

There was a long silence.

'No,' said Sapphire at last.

'This will sound so cold and business-like,' said Angie Vaze, 'but really it's the most kind and simple solution all round – for you, me and, most important of all, for the baby.'

Sapphire and the woman looked at each other.

'I'm offering you a way out. And a settlement. Ten thousand pounds as compensation – not payment, that's so crude – as a gesture of thanks.'

Sapphire glanced at her mother and sister.

'You want to buy the baby,' she said.

'I *long* for a baby,' Angie Vaze repeated. 'It would complete my life. But it would,' Angie bit her lip again, 'wreck yours. If we could come to some agreement,' she glanced at Jude, 'you would all have the peace of mind of knowing that the baby would be brought up by someone who would love it to death – to bits – and would give it everything.'

'It's a way out,' said Miranda.

The three women looked at Sapphire.

'I'm really not sure,' said Jude, as Sapphire said nothing. 'But it's a thought.'

The hot, heavy air carried the distant sound of sirens into the room. Sapphire glanced over her shoulder to look out of the window.

'Sapphire,' snapped Miranda. 'Pay attention.'

Sapphire pulled her mind back into the room.

'What?'

'What do you want to do?' said her mother.

'I don't know,' said Sapphire. She dug her nails into her palms. 'I want to go out.'

Angie Vaze's face twitched.

Jude sighed. 'Oh, Sapphire. Can't you be a bit more grown up about this?'

'Well, I don't know, I don't know, I DON'T KNOW!' yelled Sapphire. 'What if I gave the baby to her then changed my mind? What if she changes her mind? What if I bumped into her in the street one day? What if – if . . .'

Jude ran a hand through her heat-flattened hair and it

sprung up on end. ‘She’s right,’ she said. ‘It’s too messy. Too many ifs.’

‘I don’t want to have it at all!’ said Sapphire.

The noise of the sirens grew louder. She looked out of the window again, scanning the roofs and treetops for a wisp of smoke. She wanted to take a run at the window and crash right through to leap over the lawns and the wall and the houses and land up next to the fire, with Gil.

Sapphire began to cry.

‘I think you should go,’ Jude told Angie Vaze. ‘I’m sorry but this isn’t going to work.’

Reluctantly, the woman stood up. Her face twitched again.

‘If you change your mind, Sapphire . . . I know how hard this is. I really do.’

Sapphire nodded then shook her head. Angie put out a hand, as if to shake Sapphire’s hand in goodbye, but as the girl continued to cry quietly, and the hand was left dangling, she withdrew and left.

‘I give up on you, Sap!’ Miranda spat out the name she always used in a fight.

‘Sorry,’ said Sapphire, clenching her teeth to stop crying.

There was a horrible silence.

‘People are trying to help you,’ said Miranda. She got up and slammed out of the room.

Jude sat down beside her daughter on the couch.

‘All right,’ she sighed. ‘We’ll sort things once and for all in the morning.’

‘Now remember – I’ll do the talking,’ Sapphire’s mother reminded her as they pushed open the door of the doctor’s surgery. She grabbed Sapphire’s hand and gave it a reassuring squeeze. ‘OK?’

Sapphire didn't feel OK; her insides were squirmy with nerves, but she nodded, feeling the cold sweat of Jude's hand in her own.

'I'm here to see Dr Devine,' Jude told the receptionist. 'I – Sapphire and I – have an emergency appointment.'

The receptionist, looking flustered, forced a smile. 'Take a seat, Mrs Dean. You might have a little bit of a wait, I'm afraid – we've had to fit in a few emergency appointments this morning.'

Jude sighed as she sat down on one of the waiting-room sofas. 'Just what I need. I can't spare my whole morning. Mrs Clayborn's poorly and you know your dad isn't good at handling things all on his own.'

'He's not on his own,' Sapphire reminded her, an edge of resentment in her voice. 'He's got matron and the care nurses.'

'On his own without me, I mean. He likes me around. He gets too emotional. Oh, hello, Amanda!' Jude switched on her smooth, bright, outside face. 'Oh, you don't look at all well.'

The too-thin woman on the opposite sofa gave a blink instead of a hello. She was so tanned she looked leather-bound. Her eyes were red and leaky. She shivered, though the waiting room was small and stuffy, and pressed her lips together as if she might leak into full flood at any second. Sapphire hadn't recognized her at first: unmade-up, her dark, bobbed hair unbrushed, her face appearing much more lined than usual, she looked so unlike her normal self.

Then the girl sitting beside the woman lowered a magazine from her face and Sapphire saw a young, fresh, golden-skinned version of the leathery woman.

Blood rushed to Sapphire's face.

Grace.

And her mother.

Perfect.

Sapphire tried to block all thought of what she and Gil had done the other night, but it didn't matter: her blazing face declared her guilt.

Grace's mother began to cry as she told the tale of what had happened to her pagoda.

'Oh, Amanda, that's *awful*,' Jude kept saying.

'I haven't slept in two nights so Ted said I had to come and get something from the doctor to calm me down. I just can't cope with this – can't sleep, can't eat, can't do anything . . . I'm *utterly* devastated. When are they going to catch this firebug, this – this *monster*? What are the police and forensics doing about it? Next we'll be burned in our beds!'

Grace shot Sapphire a glance.

'I'm sorry,' Sapphire blurted, wishing she could hide her burning face.

Grace shrugged.

'Me too,' she said quickly. She examined her nails. 'About – you know.'

Grace was sorry? About what? About stealing Jay?

Sure you are, thought Sapphire. If Grace really felt bad about stealing people's boyfriends, how come she kept on doing it? No, Sapphire decided, noting the other girl's unusual tenseness – the way Grace continuously flicked her hair, chewed her lip and picked at the embroidery on her jeans. The jeans made her look twice. Grace had outlawed that particular style. Embroidered denim was *so* last year, she'd said. If Grace didn't care that she was wearing last year's jeans then things must be bad.

But she wasn't so much sorry, Sapphire reckoned, as

embarrassed. Sitting here face to face with someone whose boyfriend she'd just stolen, with her dishevelled, sniffling mother beside her, instead of bodyguarded by her usual acolytes. It must be killing her, thought Sapphire, with satisfaction.

'Oh, him,' said Sapphire. 'Forget it. You're welcome to him. Can't stand him any more.'

Jude turned.

'Who?' she snapped.

She stared hard at Sapphire, then at Grace. 'Who were you talking about?'

Grace darted a quick, nervy glance from Jude to Sapphire.

'No one,' muttered Sapphire.

Jude absorbed the high colour of Sapphire's cheeks.

'Maybe Grace will tell me who this boyfriend of yours is, if you won't,' said Jude, then looked as if she'd like to bite off her own tongue as she remembered the reason for their visit to Dr Devine was top secret, and the last person she'd want to know about it was Amanda Matters. 'Thinks she's really something, that one,' Jude always grumbled whenever she bumped into Grace's mother. 'Always so smug, the way she goes on and on about what she's bought for her wonderful house this week, looking down her nose at me because we don't own our own home.'

Grace darted quick, butterfly glances, trying to work out what was going on. As she lifted her arm to flick back her hair for the umpteenth time, Sapphire saw two red parallel lines on the inside of her arm. Raw cut lines.

Seeing her stare, Grace quickly slammed her hand on to her knee, wrist down.

No one knew why Grace cut herself. She hadn't done it all summer. Her body had been on display in the skimpiest of tops and shorts; smooth, tanned and perfect. But last winter, everyone had whispered about the mess of her arms and her ankles, whenever they'd changed for gym at school.

'I just can't get over it,' Mrs Matters sobbed, yet again. 'My beautiful pagoda. I've completely lost my peace of mind.'

'You'll get it back,' muttered Grace, 'just as soon as Dad buys you a new one.'

Amanda Matters turned on her daughter.

'You're such a hard, cold little bitch, Grace. You don't care about me at all – you never give a damn about what I'm going through, what I have to cope with in life . . . all you ever think about is yourself. It's all you, you, you. What about me? Why can't you ever think about me? I don't know why I ever had you. My life was perfect until you came along!'

Sapphire heard the sharp intake of her own mother's breath as Amanda Matters turned away from her daughter, hugging her arms around herself.

Grace just closed her eyes but Sapphire saw her fists and jaw clench as her mother ranted on and on about her selfish daughter and the loss of her precious pagoda.

Suddenly Sapphire could see why the ruin of the pagoda, her intended revenge, had been a gift to Grace; and why someone like Grace, who appeared to have everything, might feel as if she had nothing. And why, with a mother like Mrs Matters, she might feel the need to grab love and attention wherever she could. Why she might be so full of anger that she might turn that anger on whoever she could – even on her own body.

And why she would smile with satisfaction as her mother's precious pagoda burned to the ground.

'Mrs Dean,' called the receptionist. 'Dr Devine will see you now.'

'We've been waiting absolutely ages,' Mrs Matters complained. She looked piqued that the Deans' emergency had pipped her own.

'How *awful* for you, Amanda,' said Jude once again. 'I'm *so* sorry.'

But as they left the waiting room, Sapphire saw the look on her mother's face. She wasn't sorry at all.

It was Dr Devine's eleventh appointment that morning and it wasn't yet ten o'clock. He was hitting his target of five minutes per patient – had actually got the last one in and out in less than four – and if he kept this up he might, for once, manage a cup of coffee and a quick cigarette with his head stuck out the open window behind his desk. It was his secret vice.

'Come in, come in,' he called out to Sapphire and her mother as they entered, then frowned distractedly over the scribble pad on his desk, to indicate how very busy he was. 'Now, what can I do for you exactly?'

It was a sharper question, he had found, than asking a patient what the problem was. A quicker way of getting to the point. Most patients didn't really care what was wrong with them, he reasoned, they only wanted the doctor to magic it all better, so it was as well just to ask what they wanted, straight off, and give it to them if possible. Nine times out of ten, it worked. At least it got them out of the surgery quicker and he could tick his target sheet, then have a five-minute indulgence of a cigarette, on a good morning.

'Well,' Mrs Dean glanced across the desk at him.

The mother was nervous, the doctor immediately saw.

And the girl – what was her name again? Dr Devine glanced at his computer screen – ah, yes, Sapphire. Silly name. The girl was looking at her feet. Dr Devine's heart sank as he mentally shredded his target sheet. He took a deep breath and tried not to let it out as a sigh.

'Better to get right to the point. Right away,' prompted Dr Devine, the thwarted desire for a nicotine boost making him sharper than he intended.

He leaned back and shut the window with a bang. Sapphire jumped at the noise and looked up from her feet.

'I'm pregnant,' she said.

Dr Devine placed his glasses on his nose then pushed them on to his forehead. 'Ah,' he said. 'And how do you know this?'

'I've done a test.'

'Hmm. What kind of a test?' enquired the doctor.

'The one with the little white stick you get in the chemist,' said Sapphire, remembering the bus journey along the Great Western Road to a city chemist where she was unlikely to bump into or be served by anyone she knew.

'And it was definitely positive?'

'Yes,' whispered Sapphire.

'Are you sure? You wouldn't happen to have kept the predictor stick so that I can have a look?'

Over the years, Dr Devine had seen girls and women who thought that a positive result meant all was well, that they weren't pregnant. Who thought that predictor sticks showing a blue line in the little window meant they would have a boy baby, and that a pink line meant a girl. Or that two lines meant twins. He had, he mused, seen it all.

'I saw it,' said Mrs Dean. 'It was definitely positive.'

'Well, let's have a look at you,' said Dr Devine, indicating the examination table.

'We want to organize a – a termination,' said Jude in the firmest voice she could muster.

Jude had decided, after last night, that her first instinct had been the right one. Sapphire's outburst to Angie Vaze had struck home. How would *she* feel if she bumped into that woman in the street, with her grandchild in a pram? How would she feel just knowing, always knowing, that the child was out there being brought up by a stranger? How did she know the woman would make a good parent? She had her high-profile career so wouldn't she just dump it in a nursery from dawn till dusk?

Jude knew how she would feel – guilty. And she'd never be able to lose the guilt or forget – the woman would always be popping up on television, wouldn't she?

Jude had also decided, after waking up at the crack of dawn and silently rehearsing the words in her imagination, that she preferred the the word termination to abortion. It sounded less – well, just less. Abortion sounded more violent, somehow.

'So you want an abortion,' said the doctor. He stared hard at his young patient as she hoisted herself up on the examination table and lay down. 'And which one of you wants this?'

'We both do,' said Jude.

Sapphire looked at the ceiling.

'Sapphire?' said the doctor.

'I . . .'

'We don't just give out abortions to anyone who might want one,' said Dr Devine. Jude flinched inside as the doctor continued to use the word, as if he knew exactly why she preferred the other one.

Which, of course, he did.

'Tell me why you couldn't have this baby, Sapphire. I don't see why not.'

Though, of course, he did.

The girl – the doctor looked at her more closely now that she was on the examination table – was hardly more than a child.

'How old are you now, Sapphire?'

'Fourteen,' she whispered.

'Do you know exactly when you had your last period?' asked the doctor, knowing she wouldn't.

'No,' said Sapphire.

'Have you any idea?'

'A couple of months ago, I think – before school broke up.'

'Good,' said the doctor, feeling her stomach. 'Can you remember how long before school broke up?'

'Not really. A little while before, I think.'

'So you're probably three months' pregnant. I wouldn't say more than four.'

'Yes.' Sapphire nodded.

'Could it be more?'

'I don't think so,' said Sapphire.

'And you don't want to have this baby. Or do you really, Sapphire? Do you know the effect an abortion might have on you? It's not like getting a tooth out.'

'Of course she doesn't want it,' said Jude.

The doctor sighed. He really should ask the mother to leave so that he could speak to the girl alone. But he had umpteen other patients to get through before lunchtime . . .

'Are you sure you know what you want, Sapphire? Have you thought about how you might feel if you abort this baby?' the doctor persisted. 'How do you think you will feel afterwards?'

He knew the child wouldn't have a clue about what she really wanted or what she might feel. How could she, at fourteen, know that? How could anyone? But it was his duty to ask.

'Do you understand, Sapphire, what abortion actually means?'

Sapphire gulped. The doctor heard her.

'I . . .'

'It means she'll get her life back,' interrupted Jude. 'She won't have it ruined by a baby she's not grown up enough to look after. She's not ready to have a baby, Dr Devine. She's still a child herself.'

'Yes,' sighed the doctor, who felt he really should put up more of a fight. He should try harder to put all the alternatives to the scared and shivering child who lay in front of him, staring blankly at the ceiling. It was his ethical duty.

Or was it? Where exactly did his duty lie? the doctor asked himself, as Sapphire slid off the examination table. He asked himself this question every time he'd found himself faced with the problem of a miserable, pregnant schoolgirl. And over the years he had faced it many times.

Pregnant schoolgirls weren't an issue in a place like Hungry, but not because young girls didn't get pregnant. Young girls got pregnant everywhere. It was what nature designed them to do. It had been happening since the beginning of time and it didn't matter how much sex education or contraceptives you threw at them, the doctor had long ago decided, young girls would always end up pregnant, whether they were ready or not.

It was human nature. The way of the world.

But human nature was at odds with the way of the world in a place like Hungry. Here, the world demanded that girls kept their aspirations high, that they didn't let human nature get in the way. It demanded that Dr Devine help the girls and their parents deal swiftly and invisibly with the problem of teenage pregnancy. Or sweep it under his carpet, magic it away and make it all better. It depended on how you looked at it.

It was his duty to do what was best for his patient, the doctor told himself. The unborn fetus wasn't his patient because it wasn't a person yet. You had to be registered as a patient to be a patient, and a fetus wasn't, so he had to do what was best for the girl. Sometimes, he didn't always know what was best. You just had to do what you *thought* best in a difficult situation and try to cover all the bases.

'What about the father, Sapphire?' asked Dr Devine, returning to his desk.

Sapphire looked at her mother. 'Oh, he – he was too busy to come today. One of the old ladies isn't well and—'

'Dr Devine means the father of your baby. She won't say,' Jude told the doctor.

The doctor nodded. Par for the course. Young girls hardly ever revealed the boy involved. Often the boy never even knew. Often the girl didn't want him to know, for all sorts of reasons – because she thought he might not want to see her again; because she didn't want the added pressure of his parents on her back when the pressure of her own was bad enough; because she might be banned from seeing him again; or because she had gone off him and didn't want him involved. Sometimes a girl would come to him alone, or with her best friend, but hardly ever with the boy involved.

The variations were endless, but nine times out of ten it all ended up the same.

'You are quite sure that you want a termination, Sapphire,' said the doctor gently, though he knew from the wretched look on the girl's face that she wasn't sure of anything at all.

Sapphire nodded, eyes again on her feet, as Dr Devine reached for the phone and punched out the number of the clinic in the city, without looking it up in the book, because it was a number he knew off by heart.

As his conversation with the clinic doctor ended and he put down the phone, Dr Devine couldn't help a quick, guilty glance at the clock. There might just be time, if his luck was in and there were no more pregnant teenagers or difficult patients this morning, for that coffee and cigarette after all.

He looked at his computer screen as Sapphire and her mother left, to see the name of his next patient.

Amanda Matters.

Dr Devine extinguished all thought of a cigarette break. His luck was out.

'Well, that's that settled,' said Jude in a voice light with relief, as they crunched up the gravel path of Hunger Home. 'We keep this to ourselves and get on as normal. Dr Devine is going to let us know when your clinic appointment is, and that'll be that.'

She waved over at Gretel who was crouched on the lawn with a little friend. Gretel and her friend spent whole days in the shade of the trees, searching the lawns for ladybirds and lucky four-leafed clovers.

Jude punched the security code into the main door intercom, then turned to Sapphire. 'I just hope you've learned your lesson because I never want to go through anything like this ever again.'

'Yes,' said Sapphire. 'I mean no.'

Boris met them halfway up the huge staircase.

'Bit of an emergency, Jude.'

'I knew it!' Jude bounded up the rest of the stairs. 'The minute I'm away . . .'

Boris put a hand on Sapphire's arm. Tentatively, she smiled up at him, but the smile froze on her lips as she saw his expression.

'I know what's been going on. I know what the two of you are up to, and I can't just stand back and do nothing, Sapphire. I won't,' he said. His hand fastened round her arm as he led her up the rest of the stairs. 'Now, there's someone here to see you. She's waiting in the living room. You go on in and see her while I help your mum.'

Boris led her right up to the living-room door.

'But who is it?' asked Sapphire. She'd seen a doctor, a priest and a woman desperate to have a child. Who could this be now?

'Sapphire!'

Another woman, one she'd never seen before, greeted her like a long-lost friend.

'Let's look at you. *What* a pretty face. You've got Dad's looks, haven't you – though I haven't met Mum yet.'

Sapphire stared at the woman.

'Hello,' she said.

'Hello, yourself. Now, you're wondering – I bet you are – who's this mad woman in my living room that I've never met before? Well, Sapphire, your dad and Father Gunn thought it would be a good idea if I came along to see you. I'm Sister Piety.'

The short, roly-poly woman, who looked nothing like a nun, in her baggy jeans and a T-shirt covered in pink dolphins, giggled. 'But everyone calls me Sister Pie. Father Gunn calls me Sister Apple Pie. He forgets everyone's name these days but he doesn't forget that!'

She giggled again and indicated her rosy apple cheeks.

'And you are Sapphire. What a pretty name.' Sister Pie sat down on the sofa and pulled Sapphire down, right beside her. 'But you've got yourself in a pickle, haven't you, pet.'

Sister Pie pinched her lips together. She leaned her head to one side and gave Sapphire a sad, concerned smile.

'I'm something of an expert in pickles of this kind,' said Sister Pie.

Sapphire glanced, puzzled, at the nun's rotund shape. She was just plump, surely. Nuns couldn't get pregnant. They weren't allowed.

Sister Pie picked up the glance and she giggled again, blushing, but now there was a shadow of annoyance on her flushed face.

'Oh, no. This,' she patted her tummy,' is due to too many chicken bhoonas, dear. Now Sapphire,' the smile dropped from her appley face, 'I'm here to help you sort out the pickle you're in. It's my job – my calling. You see, the church runs a scheme—'

'It's all right,' Sapphire cut in. 'Dr Devine's already sorted things.'

Sister Pie recoiled.

'When did this happen?' she asked, sounding suddenly breathless.

'Well, it hasn't happened yet,' stumbled Sapphire. 'Mum and I went to see him this morning—'

'Aah.' Sister Pie's composure returned but a quiver in her apple cheeks made Sapphire wish she'd kept her mouth shut.

'Dr Devine's way of sorting things,' Sister Pie spoke carefully, 'is often not the same as ours. His solutions – well, let's say he can be misguided at times, although I'm sure he means well. Even the best doctors . . . well, they shouldn't try to play God, Sapphire.' Sister Pie grasped Sapphire's hand. 'Listen to me, dear. I want to tell you the story of a baby, a tiny baby, just hours old. This baby, a little girl, was left in a shoebox in a bus shelter. Imagine, Sapphire, a shoebox!'

Sister Pie's apple cheeks deepened to plums. 'She was abandoned, this little one, left to fate, left to *die*, perhaps. And she might have died, if she hadn't been found in time by a nun who had come out of a nearby church to wait for her bus. That baby, Sapphire – can you guess who that baby was?'

The rapturous look on Sister Pie's face made Sapphire think of angels, of the baby Jesus.

'That little baby . . . was me.'

'Oh,' said Sapphire.

'So you see,' Sister Pie continued, 'that's why I'm here to help you today. God made sure that I was saved and this is my thank you to Him – to make sure no other babies are lost that could be saved.'

'Have you spoken to my mum?' ventured Sapphire, wondering what she would have to say about all of this.

'I've spoken to Dad and he's very concerned, Sapphire. Dad loves you so much.'

'But Mum—'

'Loves you just as much and has had a very nasty shock and doesn't quite know what to do for the best. Mum is in a panic and has rushed into something.'

You haven't even met her, thought Sapphire resentfully.

'But there is another way, Sapphire, a better way to deal with this. You do not have to kill your own baby. You mustn't. What a terrible thing to do. But with help, you can easily keep your baby. That's what I'm here to do – give you the help you need.'

'But it's all been decided,' said Sapphire. 'I don't want to keep it.'

Sister Pie sighed. She pulled out a green folder from the large straw bag at her feet.

'Has anyone explained to you exactly what abortion is, Sapphire? I don't suppose you know anything about the horrors of the evacuation of the uterus, and why should you? So let's have a look.'

Sister Pie pulled out some photographs from the folder and passed them silently, one by one, to Sapphire.

Sapphire felt sick. She wanted to run out of the room, to escape Sister Pie and her horrendous photos. She started to tremble.

Sister Pie sighed again and put the photos away.

'I don't enjoy doing that, Sapphire, but you have to know. Now let's think more positively. There's money and support available from the Church for young girls like you, to help you buy the things you need for the baby and to give you someone to talk to whenever you need. There's always someone like me on the end of a phone. I'm going to leave you to have a little think and then I'll come back and we can have another talk, with Mum too, and we'll see how things are. All right?'

Sister Pie put her arm across Sapphire's shoulder and gave her a crushing hug. 'I know this is hard, Sapphire, and I really want to help you do the right thing. It's not just you to think of though, there's a baby too – an innocent baby. But I don't believe in lost causes. Now, chin up, don't fret. You're not the first girl in the world to be in this pickle and unfortunately you won't be the last. Let's talk again tomorrow. OK?'

'OK,' said Sapphire.

Sister Pie gathered up her photos and slipped them back in their folder. She brought out one last one and placed it on the table with a smile.

'That's a happier pic – one of our young mothers and her little tot.'

Sister Pie grabbed her bag and left.

What a wonderful place for a little one to grow up and play in, she thought, as she crunched down the gravel path. Look at the lawns and trees! Look at the space! It wasn't as if the girl lived in a high-rise flat in a rundown, drug-ridden place like many of the pregnant teenagers she saw. This girl had everything. A mother *and* a father. A nice, caring one too. So many of the girls she counselled came from broken families. Some girls had never known their father, or hadn't seen him for years – he had run off with someone else or was in jail – or the father was a drunken wreck. Sometimes the girl's mother was just as bad.

That was hard, bringing a baby into all that. Of course it was. She could see that. But life *was* hard, sometimes; you still had to put the unborn baby first.

These scared, upset young girls wanted an easy way out. Just as her own mother had. But no matter how scared and upset, you could not leave a baby in a shoebox to die or, if it was lucky, for someone else to find and bring up. Neither should you give it away to strangers. Or kill it in a clinic. Then get on with your own life as if nothing had happened. Sister Pie closed the gate and took one last glance behind her at the palatial mansion and its vast grounds. However sorry she felt for the girls – and she did feel for them, she *did* – under no circumstances should you ever get rid of a baby. A baby was precious and should be kept safe and cherished by its mother.

And Sapphire Dean had everything going for her.

Sister Pie hurried to catch the bus she could hear rumbling round the curve of the hill. In her rush to stick out her hand to halt the bus, she barged into the wisp of a woman who stood inside the shelter, murmuring shreds of a poem like a prayer.

Too out of breath to speak, Sister Pie grasped the woman's arm in a brisk gesture of apology, an action which caused the woman to cry out in alarm and run off.

It's a funny old world, full of funny folks, thought Sister Pie, as she often did. But that was the way God had made it. All you could do was try to make things right.

I'll save that precious little life, she vowed, as she stepped on to the bus. I'll save that baby just as the nun once saved me.

'How are we all on this fine day, folks?' Boris called into the TV lounge, as he passed by on his way to his office.

He wasn't really asking, just letting them know he was around. The old folks were engrossed in a TV hospital drama, enjoying the on-screen battles of life and death, while their own bodies continued their struggle against time.

Boris made himself stop, go back and pull the window blinds down against the sun, so that they could see the TV screen better. As he did so, he saw the bright pink blob of Sister Pie's dolphin T-shirt vanish into the trees on the far edge of the grounds.

It brought to mind an image of Sapphire in the bright, clingy tops she'd worn with denim shorts all summer. Always busy, he had only half-noted the precociously adult look of the clothes, the nail varnish and lipgloss, the hair gel and chewing gum. To him, it had all made her look just as much of a little girl as ever. She was still his little princess, he'd thought; just play-acting, dressing up like the big girls, pretending to be a grown-up princess.

He'd been wrong. He hadn't even known she'd had a boyfriend, he thought guiltily.

Boris pictured her in the arms of some boy. He felt unnerved, betrayed by the fact that his little girl had transformed overnight, it seemed to him, into a young woman he wasn't sure he knew. A young woman who'd had sex. Boris turned away from the thought.

Today, taking Father Gunn's advice and asking Sister Pie to come and talk to Sapphire, he had only done what he thought best. And Jude was doing the same. They were at stalemate.

'What's up, son?'

The voice next to him interrupted his thoughts.

'Life, Jack, life,' said Boris. 'Don't ever have a teenage daughter.'

Jack Stirling wheezed out a laugh. He was almost eighty. He might not last the winter, Boris knew, with that weak chest of his. A bad cold could see him off. Yet there was also a surprising strength in him.

'Where are we docking today then, Jack?'

Jack had been a merchant seaman. But dementia, combined with a strong imagination, had decided him, from the day he arrived, that Hunger Home was a great ship sailing the world's oceans.

Now Jack screwed up his eyes and peered towards the window. 'I think we'll make Massachusetts by sunset, Captain.'

Boris smiled. More and more these days, Jack was far away, journeying alone across imaginary seascapes, while those around him were stuck in the landscape of Hungry.

Over the seven years that Jack had been at Hunger Home, Boris had grown to look on the old man almost as a father and often, on a long day, would hitch a ride on Jack's fantasy ship.

When Boris was all of twenty-two and the man he'd thought was his father had just died, his mother told him, out of the blue, that she thought his real father was probably someone else. She'd once had a fling, she said. The father he'd had – the one he grew up thinking of as his father – had been kind and loving, but he was a silent, self-contained man; the kind you could never really get close to. And so the idea of his real father, the man he might have been close to if he'd ever known him, had haunted Boris's imagination all of his adult life.

The only thing he knew of his real father was that he'd been a merchant seaman. Just as Jack Stirling had been. But dementia had made a ghost of Jack's past, and whenever Boris tried to determine the details of his life, the old man's memory would flutter and fade, giving only infuriating glimpses. And there were no clues in his few possessions either.

This old man could have been my father, Boris often told himself, though he knew how unlikely that was. Almost impossible, but not quite. The fact that there was no physical resemblance between them didn't mean anything – Boris took his looks after his mother's side of the family. No, it was the bond he felt he shared with this old man that made him want it to be true.

And that's why Boris could not stomach what his wife and daughter were doing. He'd spent half his life wanting the father he never knew. How could they – and how could he let them – think about destroying Sapphire's baby, when that child belonged here in his own family?

He couldn't tell Jude why he felt so strongly. He'd never told anyone his secret. The closest he ever got was his choice of Sapphire's name. His mother had refused to give him the man's name and the only clue he had was a snapshot he found, after she died, hidden away in the back of her wallet. It was a photo of a ship with a throng of uniformed seamen waving hello or goodbye; you couldn't tell. The only thing Boris knew about the man his mother thought was his father was the name of his ship: the *Sapphire.*

He never got round to telling Jude about the name. And he felt a secret, subversive thrill when he managed to persuade her it was perfect for their blue-eyed little baby. The name had no resonance of gin-soaked nights then for Jude. All that came later, after Gretel. And though he would never have admitted to loving any one of his girls more than the others, there had always been a special closeness with Sapphire that he liked to think came from the secret link she shared with his unknown father.

That was why it felt like such a betrayal to discover that he didn't have the special bond with Sapphire that he'd believed. He didn't really know her after all, did he?

As far as Jude knew, Boris's father was dead, followed several years later by his mother, and that was that. He hadn't spoken about the confusion over his father because he felt ashamed. Ashamed for his mother and shamed at his preference of the unknown fantasy father, the one who had never been there for him, over the good, imperfect man who had brought him up as his own.

Well, he wasn't going to start telling anyone about it all now. Boris was not one to spill out his deepest secrets to the world, or even to his own wife. He'd kept his story to himself all this time, so what was the point? He couldn't change the past. He would never know who his real father was, would never come to terms with the idea that there might be someone out there – if he was still alive – who didn't know or care that he had an estranged son in the world; he could never salvage any of that. He couldn't even salvage the name of Jack's ship from his fog of dementia. But he could salvage this situation. He could make sure the right thing was done.

And surely the right thing was to protect the unborn great-grandchild of his lost father?

Sapphire was hot, cross and bored. Trapped in her room, she had only left it to sneak down to the kitchen a couple of times, and each time she was met with the flashing light of the answering machine. Emma had been ringing and ringing. Dad had forbidden her to ring back, but she didn't want to anyway after the other day.

Gretel's lice comb caught her eye and she kept herself occupied for a good half-hour, combing through her own hair, just in case. Staring at herself in the wardrobe mirror as she combed through her long, thick strands, Sapphire wondered why she didn't look any different. She turned sideways. Apart from a slight filling out of the curves of her body, which she liked – and even that was normal, she was still growing – there was absolutely no sign that she was pregnant. It would have been so easy to ignore the missed periods; but last month she had become uneasy because she had known all along that she'd been kidding herself that what she and Jay had been doing held no real risk.

Hooked on the rush of excitement, she had refused to think of the consequences. She never suggested taking precautions because she didn't want to kill that excitement. If they had started to plan and be careful, it would all have been spoilt.

It was well spoilt now.

But what about Jay? What had he told himself? He had been carefree, as if responsibility for what they were doing was all down to her. He seemed so confident that she wouldn't take a risk with her own future.

He shouldn't have been so trusting.

But then, he had been right. Events proved that it wasn't anything to do with him. None of this nightmare had touched him.

Sapphire flung down the comb, made her hand into a fist and punched her stomach. She punched again, harder, trying not to tense against the blow. Maybe, if she kept going, she could punch this pregnancy out of existence. She kept punching, as hard as she could until she was sore and out of breath. And waited to see what would happen.

There was the tiniest fluttering, like the beating of wings. An unnerving sensation at the very core of her, as if the tiny being inside was fighting back, claiming its right to live.

Sapphire rubbed her sore stomach.

'I'm sorry, I'm sorry,' she whispered.

She understood. They were at odds. She and the baby were fighting for their own lives. Sapphire had just begun to spread her wings when, it seemed, she had turned upon herself and torn them off.

Now the baby inside her had started to grow its own wings.

She sat on the floor, letting the pain fade and trying not to give in to the urge to cry. She had to do something. If she sat up here in her tower room all day, she'd lose her mind. She got up and warily opened the door.

If Mum or Dad caught sight of her, Sapphire knew she'd be given a horrible task like pushing a smelly laundry trolley round the corridors, collecting dirty bedlinen. Her only other option was the reading room, so she sneaked downstairs.

At the door, she stopped and peered in. This room, more than any in the house, had retained some of its past grandeur. It was huge, with a high, ornately plastered ceiling, picture windows and a great sheen of original oak floor. Once a ballroom, this was where the sugar lord had held vast parties; now it was crammed with armchairs and sofas full of old people. Yet it was so quiet you'd hardly know. They were asleep.

Tiptoeing across the room, Sapphire secreted herself behind the thick pink drapes of a window-seat, sacrificing the cooling air of the ceiling fan for some welcome but stuffy privacy. She reached across the window-seat and took a magazine from a pile.

Only old Mrs Merry was still awake; all the other old folk in the room were drooped in their seats. The massive ceiling fan that Boris had installed in the reading room was their best means of escape from the assault of afternoon heat. The small, plug-in fans in the bedrooms and TV lounge were too feeble to do more than stir the air so, as soon as lunches were over, there was a mass rush to grab a seat in the cooling grandeur of the reading room.

Sapphire flicked through the magazine, half-reading make-up and diet tips, though her mind was really on a volume in the bookcase near the fireplace, on the top shelf above the bulging stacks of romantic novels and thrillers. It was a well-thumbed medical book. But she'd wait, Sapphire decided, until Mrs Merry was safely asleep.

Which might be a while, she saw with a sinking heart as

the old woman spied her and began to shuffle over for a chat. Sapphire put her nose in the magazine and made a show of being engrossed.

'What's that you're reading?'

Mrs Merry liked a chat and was not easily put off. The tiny, meringue-haired old woman squeezed in beside her on the window-seat.

'Oh, just—'

With a jolt Sapphire saw what the article was about. Mrs Merry leaned across before Sapphire could turn the page.

' "A new study reports that most women who have terminated a pregnancy suffer no adverse reactions or psychological trauma," ' Mrs Merry read with interest. She nodded. 'Well, most people get over most things, don't they,' she stated placidly. She prodded Sapphire on the arm. 'Your generation think they invented trauma. I lost my husband *and* my lover within months of each other in the Second World War.' She lowered her voice to a confidential whisper. 'Found out I was pregnant and didn't know whose it was. Couldn't face having it. I wanted to get out and live a bit.'

Sapphire blinked. Mrs Merry looked at her sideways.

'Wasn't easy to get an abortion in those days, but there's always a way to do what you need to. So there I was, no husband, no lover, no baby. But I kept myself together and decided just to get on and live my life – though I wasn't really happy at first. That took a bit of time.'

Why was Mrs Merry telling her this? It was as if she knew something. But how could she?

Then Sapphire remembered that the old woman had been hanging on Dad's arm when he had pulled the predictor stick out of Rose Wolfbane's mouth. She must have heard something of the rumpus afterwards. Knowing Mrs Merry, she would have followed them upstairs to see what was going on. Mrs Merry was always snooping about, wandering into their living quarters and places she wasn't supposed to be. She was always complaining that she wanted some real company because she was fed up with all these old folks.

Sapphire's day of imprisonment had given her a painful awareness of what it might be like to spend your days stuck inside the Home. She looked at Mrs Merry with new sympathy. And decided to chance a difficult question.

'Didn't you ever wish that you hadn't got rid of the baby?'

'Oh, no,' she said. Then paused. 'Well, maybe I did sometimes. Some things are never clear cut, black and white. Sometimes you have regrets whatever you do. But it would have been a mistake to bring a baby into my life then, the horrible way I was feeling. I wouldn't have been a very good mother. No, I was just like those women,' she tapped the magazine, 'the Two Out Of Three who got over it and got on with their lives. Same as lots of other women back then because it wasn't just me – oh, no! Having that baby would have wrecked me just then. Later on, I had babies. Those three big lumps,' the old woman raised her eyes to the ceiling, 'that remember to come and see me once in a blue moon.'

Mrs Merry looked at Sapphire keenly. 'I'm a nosy old pest and I sometimes hear things I shouldn't.'

'So you – you know?' whispered Sapphire.

Mrs Merry nodded and put a finger to her lips. 'But I can keep a secret.'

Unexpected tears stung Sapphire's eyes.

'Now, now,' said Mrs Merry and she took Sapphire's

hand between both of her own. 'I know you, Sapphire. I've known you since you were little. And I know that you've got what I had – you've got oomph. A girl with oomph can get over even the worst thing and doesn't let it ruin her life. She gets on with living. And you *must*,' Mrs Merry clasped Sapphire's hand tighter, 'because life is a lot shorter than you think. You're old before you know it!'

Mrs Merry gave a sudden yawn. 'Not that there's much oomph left in me these days, eh?' She smiled. Sapphire scrubbed her eyes and gave back a watery smile. 'Just remember, most people get over most things. It all fades.' The old woman yawned again. 'Nap time for me.'

Once Mrs Merry had returned to her armchair, Sapphire studied the magazine article; every word. Then she went over to the bookcase and lifted down the medical encyclopedia that she and Miranda used to sneak up to their bedroom and pour over in secret.

She took it back to the window-seat and looked up the section on 'Giving Birth'.

Sapphire was so engrossed that she only heard the familiar rattle and squeak of Gretel's roller skates a second before her young sister crash-banged through the door of the reading room and bashed to a stop behind a sofa, causing several of the oldies to jolt in their sleep. Sapphire didn't even have time to slam the book shut.

Gretel skated over to the window-seat. Her nose and forehead were beaded with sweat.

'Eeeyuks! What's *that*?'

She stuck out her tongue and made sick noises as she leaned over to see the photographs in the book.

'Ssh!' Sapphire nodded a warning towards all the sleeping old people. But Gretel was too fixated by the photographs to care.

'That's *disgusting*.'

Skates clattering, Gretel jumped on to the window-seat beside Sapphire. 'What is it?'

'Never you mind,' said Sapphire, shutting the medical book.

But Gretel had her hand in the page and she flicked it back open. 'Is that a lady having a baby? Is it? Is that its *head*? Oh, yuk!'

Sapphire snatched the book away.

'Aw,' complained Gretel. 'Let me see more. Why can't I see more?'

''Cause it's horrible,' said Sapphire. 'Will you shoosh?'

One of the old men in the armchairs harrumphed like a horse in his sleep.

'Lots of things are horrible,' said Gretel. 'Slugs and things like toilets. But you need slugs and toilets. Horrible things aren't so bad when you look at them for a while. Then you get used to them. Let me *see* the slimy baby.'

'No,' said Sapphire, angling the book out of Gretel's line of vision. But Gretel snuggled up, trying to weasel the book from her fingers.

'Are you still infested?' asked Sapphire, shifting her head away from her sister's.

'Daddy says I've been deloused till my pips squeak. Let me see, Sapphy.'

Sapphire sighed and let Gretel open the book. She wanted to close her eyes and empty her mind of the images – but she had to look again.

The photos were as gruesome as the photos Sister Pie had shown her of abortions and dead fetuses. Childbirth and live babies looked just as horrendous. Gretel flicked through brutal page after page, until she came to a beautiful image. Sapphire stared as Gretel breathed heavily over the photo of a ghostly, alien creature, almost transparent, its head too big for its body, curled up tight like a sea horse as if it was frightened of the outside world.

The fetus at ten weeks.

That's what's inside me, that little sea horse, thought Sapphire.

'I want to see the baby coming out again,' said Gretel, flicking back the pages to find it. 'The mummy looks like she's in *agony*. D'you think it's worse than getting a filling? I'm never having a baby if it is. Is it, Sapphy?'

Sapphire looked at the woman in the photo and felt her insides slide.

'Looks like it,' she said.

The ceiling fan whirred uselessly. The hot, heavy air in the reading room was infused with the sweet and sour scents of sweat and talcum powder, soggy incontinence pads, old slippers and the marshmallow cakes that the old people liked with their afternoon tea. The peculiar mix reminded Sapphire of the smell that hung at the back of the walk-in toy cupboard when they were little – where Gretel's discarded nappy would lie beside broken jammy dodgers, odd shoes and a musty pile of dressing-up clothes.

Once again, Sapphire's eyes stung with tears. She pushed her face into her little sister's hair.

'Mum,' said Gretel. 'Mummy.'

Gretel leaned over the back of the sofa and prodded her mother's arm.

'Gretel, darling,' Jude turned round. 'Go and tell Sapphire to come downstairs.'

Gretel looked from her mother to the woman who was sitting at the other end of the sofa.

'But Mum . . .'

'On you go.'

'But Mummy, she *is* downstairs. She's in the reading room and she's crying.'

'Oh.'

Jude turned back to the woman with a relieved smile. 'Oh, dear. Well, I'm afraid we'll have to leave things for now. Things are difficult – it's been a very difficult day.'

'Of course,' said Angie Vaze. 'I just wanted to let you know that I'm willing to raise my first offer.'

'First offer?' Jude looked blank.

'After discussing things with my husband we decided that what I'd first suggested, you know, financially – well, it wasn't realistic so I'm very willing to—'

'I'm sorry,' Jude cut in, 'but we went to see the doctor today—'

'Is there a problem?' Angie Vaze leaned forward in her seat. 'With the baby, I mean?'

'No, it's just that we've decided that Sapphire is going to have a termination,' said Jude. 'The doctor decided it was the best thing for her.'

'I see.' Angie Vaze looked as if she was going to burst into tears. 'And the fact that I'm willing to love and adore that child, and give it every chance in life, and not only that but I'm offering Sapphire a settlement that could be a stepping stone to all sorts of opportunities – all she has to do is see the pregnancy through and deliver a healthy baby – that doesn't make you think again? Why destroy the life of a child that someone else desperately, desperately wants? Why not give your daughter a better chance too? It's only a few more months of her life.'

Jude rubbed her forehead. Suddenly, though it was only late afternoon, she felt desperate for a drink. A nice, cold gin (she imagined the ice clinking against the glass) would calm her and help her deal with things. It was all getting too difficult.

Jude smiled at the other woman, though she was getting on her nerves. 'Why don't we talk about this over a drink? It's so hot. Why not join me in a gin and tonic – just a little one – and we'll talk this out.'

'Lovely,' said Angie Vaze, who hated the very smell of gin – it was like drinking aftershave.

But she'd swallow petrol if it meant she'd have a chance of getting this baby.

Neither woman noticed the small figure who had slipped, unnoticed, behind the sofa and was sitting, sucking her thumb, listening to every word that was said.

Boris rubbed the palms of his hands down the sides of his shirt and wiped his face with a sleeve before he opened the front door. It wasn't just the heat that had soaked him in sweat. It was the intrigue going on in the living room.

He'd walked in on Jude and the TV woman and sensed immediately that whatever was going on had something to do with Sapphire. He had come straight from the kitchen, intending to storm in and confront Jude with the message he'd just heard on the answering machine. Doctor Devine's receptionist had asked Jude to please phone back as soon as possible and confirm an appointment for Sapphire with a Doctor Gentles at some clinic in the city. Boris could guess what kind of a doctor and what kind of a clinic.

Yet there was his wife, up to something suspicious with the TV woman, he could tell.

Boris had said nothing to the two women, just rushed into the kitchen and grabbed the phone. He needed some moral support and he could only think of one thing to do.

He was outnumbered and intimidated, he knew, by those two women brewing up plans about the life of his unborn grandchild, in his own living room.

Father Gunn – after Boris had quickly reminded him of who he was and what the problem was – said he and Sister Pie would be there immediately. And they were.

'It's not the first time a family has been torn apart by this sort of thing,' said Sister Pie. Her apple cheeks were florid. She was ready for battle.

Boris sighed with relief. He turned to the priest as they climbed up the main staircase to their living quarters.

'Would you like a—'

Beer, he was about to say to Father Gunn, then caught himself. He didn't want them to think, with Sapphire pregnant and the two women flinging back gin in the living room, that the old people in his care lived in a place of ill-repute. But the priest looked as if a beer was just what he was in need of.

'*Tea* would be lovely,' said Sister Pie. 'But let's enter the lion's den first and do what must be done.'

Father Gunn's face dropped. Boris cleared his throat. He wiped his hands on his shirt and showed them into the living room.

Sapphire's heart had sunk the moment she entered the living room and saw her mother with Angie Vaze.

'Sapphire, come and sit down.'

Sapphire wanted to about turn and walk out, but in her moment's hesitation Jude reached out, grabbed her daughter's arm and pulled her down on to the sofa, in the space between herself and Angie Vaze. Sapphire had only come along to the kitchen to get a drink of water, to calm herself after her tears in the reading room, when Gretel had burst out of the living room and said Mum wanted her, right now. Sapphire had just listened to an answering-machine message. It came on the tail of a flurry of tearful messages from Emma. On her way out of the kitchen, she'd bumped into Dad, who had obviously heard it too. And the look on his face, as he picked up the phone, told her that he knew Emma knew about her pregnancy.

It was all getting out of control.

Now Sapphire, who had been trapped indoors all day, found herself sandwiched on the sofa between two tipsy and determined women.

'I want to tell you something, Sapphire.'

Angie Vaze leaned across the sofa and patted her knee. The unaccustomed gin, a Jude-sized gin, made her sway and she gripped Sapphire's knee to steady herself.

'Let me tell you,' she spoke with exaggerated care, 'what once happened to me. How I got to be in the mess I'm in. You see, Sapphire, once I was just like you. Pregnant. And I had an abortion. I'm not saying it was right but I was just out of university and had landed a job in television. A *fantastic* job. It felt like I'd just won the lottery. So I had to get rid of the baby – I had to. I couldn't have it; there wasn't time. I'd have lost my job and a chance like that only comes around once. And really,' Angie paused and her eyes seemed to unfocus for a long moment, 'really, it *was* the right thing to do, wasn't it, because I wouldn't be where I am now. But when the time came to have a baby, it didn't happen like I planned. It just didn't happen. Sometimes I wonder if the abortion damaged me, though they say it's unlikely. They say . . .' she sighed, 'it's just one of those things. I left it too late, Miranda.'

'Sapphire,' corrected Sapphire. 'My name's Sapphire.'

'But *you* don't have to make the same mistake,' Angie swept on. 'You can make everything right—'

'But you didn't,' Sapphire interrupted, 'think it was a mistake before. It's only now that you can't have a baby that you think it was.'

Angie Vaze looked at Sapphire and her eyes hardened.

'What?'

'So why can't I do what you did?' said Sapphire. 'And you were much older. What age were you?'

Angie continued her hard stare. 'Look, Sapphire, I've always been a high-achiever. I would have been a fool to lose what I had achieved when I fell pregnant. Do you have that to lose? What have *you* got to lose? A year at school? You can easily catch up on that. Now, listen, I've raised my price substantially. I'm offering you a serious amount of money. Do the smart thing, Sapphire. That's what I did. The smart thing. Then everyone's happy.'

Sapphire took in the twitch of need at the woman's mouth. She saw her dig the sharp heel of a shiny sling-back shoe into the carpet. An image flashed to mind of the delicate, curled-up sea horse creature inside her. She saw the tiny, glass-like sea horse crushed by that hard spike of heel.

I don't like her, thought Sapphire.

'No,' she said, and stood up.

Angie Vaze stood up too, blocking her exit.

'Mum,' said Sapphire. Jude was staring up at them, in an uncertain, useless way, as if she'd lost track of what was happening.

All of a sudden Sapphire felt queasy. The smell of gin, the heat and the woman blocking her route to the door were too much. It would serve Angie Vaze right if she threw up all over her silk blouse.

Sapphire glanced over her shoulder at the tower window.

Or there was that. That would show them. That would be a way out. If she took a running jump and crashed right through.

'Sapphy,' whispered a little voice.

She looked down and saw Gretel's worried face peering out from the side of the sofa, where she was crouched like a cat.

Then the door opened and Sister Pie pushed in past Dad with Father Gunn right behind.

'My wife is wrong,' Boris announced. Nerves and anger had overcome his embarrassment and he had lost his self-control.

Her father was angrier, Sapphire saw, than she'd ever known him before.

'She wants,' Boris continued, 'to sell an unborn baby that is part of *my* family to this woman. Or to abort it. I don't have a say, though it's my family too. I don't even get to know the name of the boy involved.'

'Darling,' Jude reached out an arm to him, but Boris ignored it, 'we're only trying to do what's best for Sapphire. Why do you keep going on about the boy? He's got nothing to do with it in the end.'

'It matters,' said Boris. 'Who he is matters to me.'

He wiped his hands on his shirt yet again. 'All right. Fine. I'm having nothing more to do with any of it. I've done all I can, Jude. You sit here and drink as much as you like until you've sorted it all out. You do what you want.'

What *she* wants? thought Sapphire.

'Dad,' she said out loud. 'Don't go.'

But he was gone.

*

'I can't stand it can't stand it, can't . . .'

Sapphire sat on the window-seat chanting the words under her breath to try to block out the sound of their voices.

For the last hour they all had talked, talked, talked. Everyone except her. The more they talked, the more their individual voices merged into a muddle. But through the muddle something clear was emerging – what they were really fighting over, Sapphire could hear quite distinctly, was not what was best for her or even the baby, though that's what they thought because that's what they all kept saying; what she could hear, above all else, was the sound of *their* wants, *their* needs.

Sister Pie grabbed Sapphire by the wrist.

'This is exactly the scenario that a young girl doesn't need. This,' she nodded emphatically at Father Gunn, 'is exactly what I've been writing about.'

She dived into her large straw bag and Sapphire flinched, hoping she wasn't going to pull out more of those horrible photographs. But Sister Pie brought out a newspaper page.

'This is a mock-up of the front page of next week's *Holy Post*,' announced Sister Pie. It tells the story of Girl X, a pregnant schoolgirl, and the pressures she is under not to keep her child. This meeting tonight,' Sister Pie, 'proves my point. Although I see I've *under*estimated the pressures. I need to illuminate them,' she looked resolutely at Angie Vaze, 'a little more. The bribe of a large cheque from people who think they should be able to buy a baby as if they were purchasing a holiday or a new car.' Now her eyes met Jude's. 'And a divided or unsupportive family. Well, what chance does a young girl—'

'Now just a minute—' Jude attempted to struggle out of the sagging sofa.

Angie Vaze was already on her feet. She cut in briskly, with a glinting eye. 'Now *that's* an idea. It's the perfect story for *Open Eye* – do you know it? The current affairs programme I present on TV? The bullying of vulnerable schoolgirls by fanatical elements in the Church . . . the interference of the Church in a young girl's personal decision—'

'Which is exactly what you're doing,' said Sister Pie. 'Interfering.'

' . . . quite a story.'

Sister Pie and Angie Vaze stood at opposite ends of the room, challenging each other.

'Now just a minute,' Jude repeated, unsteadily. 'That's my daughter.'

'She wouldn't be identified,' Angie Vaze said, without taking her eye off Sister Pie. 'She would be Girl X.'

Sapphire snatched the newspaper mock-up from Sister Pie and read the headline.

FORCES AT PREY ON GIRL X.

GIRL X. That's what she was now. An ex-girl. A girl who had lost herself, who was an X, not a person. An X that signified that her life had all gone wrong.

An ex-girl – a body with a baby growing inside. She had become a battleground. She didn't own her body any more. It belonged to the baby as much as to herself. That little alien stranger who was curled up like a sea horse, expecting her to protect it from the outside world.

Well, how could she? She wasn't even able to protect herself in her own home.

She felt dizzy. The roomful of faces swam.

Mum leaned forward, put out a hand, concern in her eyes.

'Sapphire.'

Sapphire pushed her mother's hand away and stepped on Angie Vaze's shiny slingbacks to get to the door. Father Gunn had been hanging around by the door, sipping the surprisingly strong gin that Mrs Dean had pressed upon him. He had not been keen to squash up on the sofa beside the other woman (he vaguely recognized her but couldn't think from where) and was convincing himself that it would be better for him to escape and leave all this to the women to sort out. He started in surprise as Sapphire barged towards him, fazed for a moment over exactly what he should do. He reacted, too late, the second after Sapphire yanked the door open and rushed out into the hall.

Sapphire ran along to the main corridor and stood at the top of the great staircase, dizzy and shaking. It would be easy. Just a missed footing, just one big jump. Then she'd be out of this, once and for all.

She stood on the top stair and swayed.

On the wall right in front, Jeanne Moreau's sultry eyes caught hers.

Life is risking.

The woman breathed the words through a voice thick with smoke. What was it, Sapphire tried to remember, that Jeanne Moreau had said the other night, from the back of the bathroom door?

Do whatever you must. Just don't stay lost.

There was a scream behind her.

'Sapphire, no!' screamed her mother. 'Oh, stop her!'

Sapphire jumped.

One big jump.

She took five steps in one go, just as Jude and Sister Pie reached out to grab her, landing on the wide corner stair. And helter-skeltered down the rest, leaping three, four, at a time, until she thumped down on to the mosaic floor of the entrance hall. Then she bolted through the main door.

Outside, she leaped the entrance stairs, stumbled, and sprawled face first in the gravel.

Panic pinned her to the ground. She lay there, too stunned to move. The sting of gravel on her hands and face brought her to her senses. She got her to her feet, dizzy and shaking.

The sound of their voices made her focus. Sister Pie's high, out-of-puff exclamations. Her mother's, cracked with despair. Father Gunn's disgruntled, awkward tones as he tried to comfort her. And the clatter of their feet on the hallway stairs.

Fear made her move.

Sapphire ran, as fast as she'd ever run in her life.

Boris got down off his ladder. He put his hedge-cutter down on the grass.

What had happened?

He watched his daughter pick herself up off the gravel and run like a hunted thing across the lawns, through the bushes and into the trees at the rim of the grounds. There was no use in calling her, he was too far away. And now she was gone.

The others burst out of the front door of the Home. They spilled out on to the entrance steps and the patch of gravel where Sapphire had fallen, pacing up and down, their heads jerking in one direction then the other.

But she was gone.

Boris sat down on the grass. What was he doing out here? Cutting the hedge?

He should have been there. Of course he should. She was still his daughter, no matter what. And he should have been there in that room to help her when she needed him most.

A small figure had emerged from the crowd at the door and was roller skating, with great difficulty, across the grass towards him. Boris groaned.

Gretel.

And from the look on her face – the same greedy, determined look she had whenever she slunk behind the living-room sofa to eat a hoard of sweeties harvested from the old folks, who spoilt her – it was clear she had grasped something of what was going on, and was on a mission to find out more.

Even with Sapphire wrapped around his imagination, Gil couldn't quite shut out thoughts of the woman who seemed, though he wasn't sure, to lurk around the edges of his life. An image of her kept creeping into his imagination. Since the other night, when he'd almost crashed into her at the bus stop, a memory had begun to resurface from his past, from before he came to Hungry; a memory of a lone figure he sometimes glimpsed at the school railings at break time, or at the end of the road as he walked home from school. The lone woman was always too far away to see clearly.

And if it was his mother, he told himself, she wouldn't stay at such a distance, would she?

Once, years ago, he remembered, he thought he'd seen a face in a gap in the caravan curtain as he lay in bed. He'd yelled in fright and Martin came hurrying in; but when his father had gone outside to look, no one was there.

After that, he never seemed to see her again.

That dowdy woman who hung around the bus stop –

she could not be the soft, smart, pretty mother he saw in his mind's eye; though he'd never really looked properly at the face of the bus-stop woman. Now that he thought about it, she was always half-turned away, her face hidden by her hair and hat. And that memory of his mother was so fragile and fuzzy that he could not trust it. There were no photos of her. He had never found one.

It had always been impossible to talk to Martin about his mother, but now Gil knew he must.

'What was she like?' he asked.

'Who?' said Martin.

They sat outside as usual. Martin was working on his saxophone, cleaning and polishing until it was the colour of clear honey and the notes ran as smooth.

Gil stretched his legs out on the grass.

'Mum.'

There was a pause, with nothing to break it except the tinkle of the wind chimes that Martin had put in the trees for Gil when he was little, to help make the barren place they'd ended up in feel like some kind of a home. There was the hint of a breeze tonight, the first in a while.

'What was her name?'

'Marie,' said Martin. He breathed on the saxophone and his polishing became fierce.

Marie and Martin Lemon. They sounded made for each other.

'Was she pretty?'

'She was,' said Martin abruptly.

Now Gil was sure he really did remember. Dark hair and eyes to match. And soft, soft skin. But no clear image. If he tried to sharp-focus the memory, it blurred and spoilt like a photograph left in the rain.

'What colour were her eyes?'

Martin flung down the polishing cloth as if it were a brick.

'Where did she go? Why did she go?' Now he was started, the questions poured out. 'Why?' Gil persisted. '*Why?*'

Martin's mouth opened and closed.

'Son, she just went,' he managed at last. 'There was some other man. Someone she once worked with. I loved her. I was happy. I thought she was happy too. But she just got up and left.'

'People don't just get up and go if they're happy.'

Martin said nothing.

'Didn't you know how she felt?'

'I never . . . I never thought about it. I just . . . I thought everything was fine.'

Gil's fingers curled around the box of matches in his jeans' pocket. So Martin had done with his mother exactly what he was doing with him now. He had ignored the obvious because he hadn't a clue how to deal with it.

How could he not notice that his son came home at night reeking of petrol and smoke? Didn't he see the obvious?

Of course he did. He just chose not to think about it. He kidded himself that everything was fine, like he had done with Mum. That was what Dad did. Not dealing with things was the way he dealt with things.

That was what had ended them up here. If Dad had gone to the boss in his old job and said, my wife's left me and I need to be around a bit more to care for my small son, wouldn't his boss have had some sympathy? But he hadn't done that. His hurt and pride, Gil figured, had made Martin struggle along, saying nothing about his personal catastrophe to anyone. His boss had lost patience with Martin taking time off, giving no good reason, and he'd lost his job.

Did not dealing with things, Gil wondered, make Dad partly responsible? If you know something is going on and you ignore it, aren't you part of its happening?

'I was only five,' said Gil. 'She promised she'd come back for me. I remember her saying it, but she never did.' He clenched the box of matches tighter. 'She promised,' he repeated. 'Why didn't she come back?'

Martin's shoulders hunched.

'Did she come back? Dad?'

The woman at the school railings and the one at the bus stop – suddenly Gil was sure they were the same person.

'Did she try to see me? Did you—'

'You've got to understand,' Martin burst out, 'that I didn't trust her any more. I'd trusted her with my happiness and what did she do with it? She destroyed it.'

Gil noticed that Martin spoke about his happiness as if he'd handed all responsibility for it over to his wife. That was a lot, thought Gil, to have to look after me and my happiness and his too. It didn't sound as if Dad had taken on responsibility for *her* happiness. He had left her to look after that too.

'She would have taken you away with her,' said Martin. 'I know that's what she wanted. I couldn't let her do that, Gilbert. You were mine. She couldn't take you and leave me with nothing.'

Gil absorbed that.

'Did she come back? And you didn't let me see her?'

'I told you, I couldn't,' said Martin. 'She kept coming back. She'd knock at the door, on and on, yelling like a madwoman. I wasn't going to let you go off with a madwoman. Not even to the park, I told her, because I couldn't trust that she'd bring you back. She wasn't fit to look after you. And no matter what she said, I wasn't letting her back in our lives just because things hadn't worked out with her new man, just so that she could hurt us all over again when she felt like it. If she could do that once, she could do it again. I wasn't going to be a fool twice in my life. So I took you away. What else could I do? I loved you – you're my son. I'd've had nothing if I'd let her take you.'

Gil remembered his mother at the window the night she left, looking out at the moon. It hadn't been a caravan window, a mucky old caravan on a wasteland. It had been a real window in a real room, in a real house. There had been a garden.

'Where did we live before? I can't remember.'

Martin glanced at the horizon. He sighed.

'Out by the coast. Gilbert, never mind that. Forget all that.'

The moon path. Gil saw the silver trail that led up to the moon. It had been moonbeams spilling all over the ocean, elongated into a shimmering ribbon of light by the waves.

'What do you think happened to her?'

The skin on Martin's face quivered.

'No doubt she's living the life she wants to now,' said Martin. 'The high life.'

Gil thought of the woman at the bus stop. 'She might have had a horrible life. Maybe it all turned out wrong.'

'And who's to blame for that?' asked Martin.

'If she came back all those times, she must have wanted me.'

'If she wanted you she would never have left you,' argued Martin.

'How long did it take her to come back?'

But Martin wasn't going to talk any more.

Maybe it was only weeks, or a few months, thought Gil. Maybe that's all it ever was. And then she came back because she couldn't be without me. Maybe she's still there, and always has been.

But the woman at the bus stop was not the one he wanted. It was the pretty mother from the past that he yearned after, not that thin, grey stranger.

That woman upset him. He didn't want her to be his mother.

Martin put his hand on Gil's shoulder as he got up.

'Time for supper, eh?'

'Not hungry,' said Gil.

'Well, I am.' Martin paused. 'You'll not be running off anywhere? I don't like the way you go out wandering at night. You don't know who's out there. That firebug's on the loose. I don't want you getting caught up in any trouble, Gilbert.' He paused again. 'Gilbert? Do you understand me?'

It was the closest Martin had come to confronting him, but it wasn't enough. Neither of his parents were enough. They would never be what he needed. So he'd just have to get himself what he needed, in the only way he knew.

Gil put a cheery smile on his face. 'I just go walking to cool down. It's too hot to sleep.'

'Yes, but—'

The rattle of a helicopter made Martin turn his head in the direction of Hungry. His face tensed. 'You're not involved in any of that, are you?'

They watched the red police helicopter circle the sky.

'No worries, Dad,' said Gilbert. 'I'm OK.'

Martin nodded.

'Be good then,' he urged.

*

She wanted to tear up the whole world; she felt as if she could.

Sapphire crashed into the sanctuary of the trees, hoping her mother and the others wouldn't try to find her here.

Everything was happening so fast.

'Gil!' she whispered. 'Gil, are you here? Please be here, please . . .'

There was no movement in the trees, not a rustle, only the clatter of a helicopter overhead. Sapphire sank to her knees in the thick of the bushes, and prayed that he would come.

Marie Bloom, who had repossessed the name she was born with, walked down the path that wound through the grounds of Hunger Home.

As soon as she had finished her cleaning shift at the Home, Marie had gone to the room she rented in the east side of the mansion. It sat right above the kitchens, and this evening's dinner – roast lamb and chocolate pudding – invaded her room with a clash of aromas that turned her stomach.

Eager to escape, she had changed her work clothes and nylon overall for the trousers and top (over-washed, faded to grey) that she always wore. She picked up the shoulder bag that gave her a purposeful look. Her only concession to the heat was to leave off her coat and socks and put on a straw hat instead of the felt one she wore in winter. Eating so little meant she was always less warm than other people and didn't feel overpowered by the extreme heat. And there was a slow grace in her movements, a Prozac-enhanced smoothness, that kept her unnaturally cool even at work.

Shaking out a pill from the bottle on the dressing table

in the bare, tidy room that was her home within the Home, she didn't so much as glance at herself in the dressing-table mirror because she didn't like the grey, dowdy woman she would see.

The room had a one-ring electric cooker and a noisy fridge, but she had unplugged both. As there was no table, she would have had to eat on the bed or at the dressing table. But she didn't really eat. She existed on strong tea, a bit of toast and biscuits from her work breaks in the Home's staff kitchen. The old people, watching her slight frame heave around an industrial-sized floor cleaner, would offer her pickings from the baskets of fruit and tins of sweets brought by relatives. She would smile at their kindness and take something to please them though she was never hungry and didn't care if she ate, didn't mind how hard or tedious her work.

In fact, she liked the cleaning work because she could do it without thinking. Her life had settled into a calm routine; all sharp edges of feeling blunted by the Prozac. The pills brought a soothing haze that felt as good as soft, summer rain. Now, she didn't worry or think about anything much, except Gilbert.

This summer, thinking about Gilbert – even with the buffer of her pills – had turned into worrying.

Bowing her head against the rising clatter of the helicopter that had begun to circle the sky over Hungry Hill, Marie Bloom hurried down the path to the entrance gate to do what she thought of as her real work in the world – her twilight shift at the bus stop, watching out for Gilbert.

She hadn't wanted her old name back. Her married name had been a link (however weak and useless) to her son. But to stay close to Gilbert in a small place like Hungry, she'd had to become anonymous.

The last twelve years had etched away her looks and her body, making her so changed she could walk past her husband in the street without him knowing it was her. Martin was still her husband; he'd never divorced her, but only because he had decided from the day she left him that she didn't exist.

Most of the time, she felt as if she hardly did.

As her hand touched the sun-warmed iron of the gate that led out of Hunger Home and into the street, Marie heard harsh, sobbing breaths. It was the sound of desperation. A sound she knew.

Through the noise of the helicopter, she heard a voice call out for Gilbert. It was the girl. And she called out his name as if he could save her.

'Gil,' she called, 'Gil.'

Marie's hand dropped from the gate. She moved towards the thicket of trees beyond the path and whispered his name into the trees too, like a spell, to make her boy come.

For the first time ever, Gil came close to being caught. His mind wasn't on the job. It was full of other things. Unfocused, he let himself be seen by the owner of the house and had to run off before the fire was even lit.

That had never happened before. The police helicopter circling Hungry for much of the evening hadn't helped.

'Gil?'

Sapphire's voice called out his name and when he heard that, he didn't care about the failed fire. He pushed through the bushes, towards her voice.

She was crouched at the foot of a tree, so crumpled up with hurt that his heart turned over.

Gil didn't know what to do.

'That fire,' she said.

He shrugged and crouched beside her. 'I blew it tonight.'

And it was all your fault, he wanted to say tenderly then reach out his hand and – then what? The rush of feeling inside pushed him even closer to her and told him what to do, but she never gave him the chance.

'The fire of all fires. You promised me.'

He had. But he couldn't be bothered with fire tonight.

'Please,' she said.

He was just thinking about reaching out his trembling hand to lift up her face and kiss her when she leaned against him and started to cry.

They climbed over the wall and ran past the bus stop.

'Sapphire!' someone called.

Sapphire heard the voice and skidded to a halt. Jay stood on the other side of the bus stop. He smiled nervously.

'You – you want to come into town? I've got money.'

'Town?' Sapphire turned right round to stare at him. 'With you?'

He walked towards her, glanced at Gil and his eyes widened. You're hanging about with *him*? his face said, and the nervous smile widened into a more confident one. Then he saw Sapphire's rigid expression and the smile dropped.

'I tried to phone you, lots of times. And then . . .'

'And then?' said Sapphire.

Jay blinked at her tone. She saw him take a deep breath. 'Grace, you know, she's hard work. Too much. A bit mad.' He shrugged and looked at her guiltily. 'Big mistake. Sorry, Sapphire, sorry.'

Sapphire began to laugh.

Jay took a step backwards.

Sapphire kept laughing; she couldn't stop. She began to run again, pulling Gil along the road with her, laughing so hard that she could hardly go on for the pain in her side and the stinging tears that blurred her eyes.

Where is there to live out here? Sapphire wondered.

'That's where I live.' Gil gestured to a place beyond the road, as if he'd read the thought. 'Over there at the back of beyond.'

They had walked to the edge of Hungry, past the last cul-de-sac where the buses turned, and now were on the long straight of the Great Western Road. The road led out into the country; when Sapphire was little she'd believed Boris when he told her it only stopped when it reached the sea.

At the side of the road was a little hill, encircled by a ring of silver birch trees. Everyone in Hungry called it the fairy ring, because of the perfect circle of trees and because, it was said, you could hear the tinkle of fairy-like music in the trees.

Gil took her hand and led her round the circle of the trees. Sapphire grasped his hand tight and stood stock still.

'Hear that?'

The faintest tinkle sounded in the trees.

'The fairy music! Listen.'

Sapphire's lips parted as the tiny sound tickled the air. She gripped Gil's hand. 'It's true then,' she said, amazed.

'The . . . what?' Gil's puzzled frown lifted and he laughed. 'No, it's just wind chimes – my dad hid them in the trees for me when I was little.'

Her face dropped and Gil wished he hadn't explained. He shouldn't have spoilt it for her.

'The whole of Hungry thinks it's fairies,' she told him.

Gil laughed again. 'Dad'll love that.'

He gestured to the caravan that sat on the edge of a

bumpy patch of wasteland. It was mostly hidden from the main road by the hill and the trees of the fairy ring. The shadow of his father's head was in one of the windows, a silhouette against lamplight.

'Here we are. Lemon Mansions.'

Sapphire stared at the caravan in surprise. Then looked around. The wasteland, with its cratered surface, had the look of a dusty moonscape.

'What's that?'

Sapphire pointed to a large ruin of a building that sat at the far edge of the wasteland.

'The East India Tyre Factory,' said Gil. 'It's still full of tyres. They used to ship the rubber from India.'

'Wow,' said Sapphire. 'All the way to Hungry.'

A petrol station by the main road, all bright lights and colour, looked out of place next to the dull moonscape of the wasteland.

'That's the petrol station my dad runs.'

He looked at her and she understood.

'I've wondered,' she said. 'About the petrol. Doesn't he notice?'

'I'm careful. I siphon off little amounts here and there.'

'If the police were any good,' said Sapphire, 'they'd have sussed you out.'

'They've been round,' said Gil. 'But Dad was my alibi.'

'What do you mean?'

'He told them I was with him at night. That all the petrol was accounted for.'

'He lied for you?'

Gil nodded.

'So he knows it's you,' said Sapphire.

Gil stared at her. 'No.'

Sapphire stared back. 'So why did he lie for you?'

'Because . . . because,' Gil struggled.

'Because he knows.'

'Because he loves me,' Gil said. 'He doesn't want to lose me.'

They stood, looking at the caravan, their hands still linked.

'The fire,' said Sapphire gently. 'If it's too dangerous, if you don't want to do it . . .'

Gil pointed to the East India Tyre Factory.

'That?' breathed Sapphire. She looked awed. 'Gil, are you sure?'

'There's a For Sale sign on it. All this – the land and the factory – is being sold to build houses on, so it'll be gone soon anyway. So will we.'

'You? 'Where'll you go?'

Gil shrugged. 'We don't know.'

Sapphire's heart dropped.

'But you'll stay in Hungry?'

'I don't know. Maybe not.'

Sapphire felt her mouth quiver. Everyone seemed to have evaporated from her life. She had distanced herself from Emma and Jay and her other friends. She had run away from her family. Gil was the only person she felt close to now. Yet she hardly knew him.

'Maybe I won't stay either,' she said.

'What trouble are you in?' Gil suddenly asked.

Sapphire pulled her hand out of his.

'I told you.'

Gil had gone over every word she'd ever spoken to him, countless times in his head, and he knew she hadn't told him. Unless it was something she'd said that very first night, when her voice had been so quiet and some things she said were drowned out by the noise of his own breathlessness and the blood pounding in his head. He shook his head but she wasn't looking at him. She was gazing at the East India Tyre Factory.

The dusk held a feeling of suspense. It seemed to focus around the ruin of the factory.

'The fire of all fires,' she whispered. 'Let's do it.'

Gil warned her that the building was unsafe, but she followed him inside as he collected petrol from his secret stash in a dark corner of the factory. Hundreds of old tyres were piled up in great dusty heaps. Tyres of all sizes; so many journeys never made.

They each took out a can and began to scatter petrol around the ruin of the factory.

It would solve all her problems, thought Sapphire, if the East India Tyre Factory came crashing down upon her head. Or if she walked into the fire of all fires, once it was ablaze. Then she'd be out of this mess she'd made of her life.

Whatever she did, whatever decision she made, someone would despise her for it. She didn't know what she was going to do but she wasn't going back home to be fought over like a scrap of meat by a pack of wolves. They didn't mean it, thought Sapphire, but that's what it felt like.

And Jay – she pictured him as she'd left him at the bus stop, his beautiful smile fading. Even then, at that most painful moment, his smile had tugged at her heart. Even then, her skin, her lips, had tingled. Even though she knew she didn't love him.

But she didn't hate him either. She had blocked him out, hadn't given him a chance. He had a right to know that she was pregnant because the tiny being inside her was part of him too. Hurt and fear – and Grace – had made it impossible.

And it was too late now.

As Sapphire scattered petrol she found herself thinking clearly, for the first time, about the option she had come to think of as the simple, difficult one. The brutal, scary one that would give her back her body and her life.

The option where the little life inside her would be ripped out, burned out of existence.

If it was so hard even to think of, how could she ever do it? And if she did, would she be one of the two out of three who coped with it, or the other one, scarred by guilt and regret?

'What happens when something burns?' Sapphire hadn't really meant to blurt out the thought.

Gil set his petrol can down for a moment.

'It turns back into atoms and molecules,' he said and wondered what lay behind her question because she sounded so broken up.

He absorbed the look on her face and continued. 'And those atoms and molecules join with others and form into something else. Ages from now, they might end up part of a star or a flower or even another person.'

'You make it sound like a fairy tale,' said Sapphire.

'It's kind of magical. You've got bits of dead star in you. So have I. Things burn up, they die, and they turn back into the building matter of the universe, like they were in the beginning, so that other things get to live. It's all a big, never-ending circle.'

Sapphire felt a ghost touch her spine. She imagined a time aeons into the future, when an atom of her own and the baby's somehow, by incredible chance, found each other again amid the vastness of the universe and joined up together to begin the life of a star, a flower or a whole new person. It would be a beautiful, unlikely, fairy-tale ending to this mess; and even if it did happen, neither she nor the baby would ever know.

It was easier to imagine how things would be if she had the baby. Not yet fifteen, she'd be caught in a limbo – the mother of a baby, yet too much of a child to really own it. She'd lose her freedom, give up her own self to give the baby a life, but the way things were going it wouldn't feel like her baby – it would belong just as much to her parents and the Church. She might as well give it up and let it be someone else's baby altogether.

But the idea of her own baby, her own child, somewhere out there, brought up by strangers – wouldn't it haunt her, forever? And the money? How could she ever enjoy that money knowing how it had been earned?

Everyone would be watching her, waiting for her to muck up, whatever she did. If she kept the baby, she'd walk down the street and her friends' parents would smile uneasily at her and her baby, thanking their lucky stars that she wasn't *their* daughter. Some days, on the way back from a long, empty afternoon in the park, she might bump into Emma and the other girls on their way back from school, and maybe they'd talk and share some of their gossip with her, while she jiggled the buggy, tired and wan-faced like the girls she'd seen outside the chip shop that night on the bus. Then they'd go their separate ways because she wouldn't be one of them any more. You couldn't be part of the girl gang when you were somebody's mum.

If she went back to school and left the baby with her mother – well, how would Mum manage the Home and the baby? She'd be so stressed out she might start drinking more and Sapphire might end up leaving school to care for it anyway.

And then, when the baby was old enough for her to get her life back, her friends would be out in the world already, away at college or university, starting first jobs, making new friends, building careers, living their lives. They wouldn't even have begun to think about having babies. But she'd still be stuck here in Hungry, in a dead-end life.

She'd be twenty-eight, her youth gone, yet so much of her own life unlived, when her child was the age she was now.

Sapphire swallowed.

'Gil, I don't know what to do.'

'What about?'

'Remember what I told you the first night I met you?'

He shook his head.

'Remember,' she urged, 'in the trees. I thought you were someone else and I told you – I told you something.'

He frowned and shook his head slowly. 'My head was buzzing from the run – you know what it's like. I couldn't really hear you. What was it?'

Sapphire put down her petrol can. She looked at Gil, puzzled. He hadn't heard? He didn't know she was pregnant? It took a moment for that to sink in.

Then he didn't have to know at all. She'd only have to tell him, Sapphire saw, if she decided to have the baby.

Gil shook out the last of his petrol.

'Paper,' he said and looked around.

'I've got paper,' said Sapphire.

Out of her pocket she took the crumpled front page of the church newspaper that she'd grabbed from Sister Pie.

She caught her breath in case he saw the headline. He

took it from her, smoothed it out before he began to roll it up, and stared.

'Hey, look.' He pointed at the page and she froze. 'It's me!' he said.

He began to laugh.

Sapphire looked. She hadn't noticed. Below the 'GIRL X' headline was a large photo of the pagoda blaze. 'IS "LUCIFER" ONE OF US?' ran the headline.

'Lucifer?' said Gil. 'What do they mean? Who's Lucifer?'

'Lucifer's the Devil,' said Sapphire, grinning.

Gil laughed again.

He crushed the page, twisted it into a long taper and handed it to Sapphire. Then he struck a match and the taper was lit.

He held it out to Sapphire. She nodded and took it.

'Throw it. Then *run*,' he said, grinning, 'like the Devil.'

Sapphire took a deep breath, stepped forward then threw the burning taper on to the trail of petrol. A moving wall of fire shot up with a force that almost blew her off her feet.

'Go!' Gil yelled, grabbing her hand.

They ran, as quick as the petrol zipped, towards the ring of trees.

There was no sign of Gilbert, or the girl.

Marie Bloom had followed them from the grounds of Hunger Home, tracking them through the streets, right out here to the very rim of Hungry, where Gilbert and Martin lived. And they had disappeared. Where had they gone? Were they in the caravan? Or inside the ruin of the East India Tyre Factory?

Marie stood in the middle of the wasteland. Out here in

the open she could be seen. Gilbert might see her. Or Martin. But the time for being careful was over.

Her son was on a course of destruction. No one except the girl seemed to know he was the firebug, and now she had joined him in his dangerous game. Playing with fire was no game, Marie knew. He thought he had it under his control but he was wrong. Fire was its own master. Gilbert was going to hurt someone. Or get himself hurt.

When she heard the girl cry out his name, she had crept into the trees and willed him to come. Then she'd listened, because she couldn't help it. She'd wanted to hear his voice. And she had. The fire of all fires, he'd promised the girl.

He had to be stopped. His father wasn't stopping him. Did Martin not see what was going on right beneath his nose? But Martin was good at not seeing. And Marie knew all too well that there was no easy way to stop someone who was all caught up in the adventure of their life.

She sat down on a pile of tyres and took off her straw hat to fan her unusually clammy face. She was worn out by a day's cleaning, by the walk, by her worries about Gilbert that had kept her awake all last night.

But just look at that sky. With her hat off, Marie had a bigger view of the outside world than usual. It was a sky of deepest blue, streaked with the fire of a setting sun. The kind of sky that once made her glad to be alive.

Two glinting silver aeroplanes were at the far edges of the evening; one flying in from the north, from a landscape of lochs and mountains, the other coming in from the western sea. They drew closer, closer, their vapour trails sketching out a vast white arrowhead across the oceanic blue. They seemed to be headed for some common point in the sky, drawn towards it like magnets. There might be a chasm as deep as a canyon between them but from down here on earth, you couldn't see.

They looked destined to crash.

Marie stopped breathing. Just for a second the two planes seemed to touch, nose to nose, wing over wing. But there was no impact. In the blink of an eye it was over, their tails parted and the planes sped safely away from each other, smoothly and silently, their vapour trails now creating a perfect white cross in the sky. Marie stood up from the pile of tyres, head bent back, mouth open, and walked round in slow, dizzying circles, gazing up in wonder at the gigantic flag that the planes had made of the sky.

The heart of the cross was right overhead.

It was a wonderful sight. Maybe it was lucky. Maybe it meant that Gilbert would be all right, after all.

She sniffed the air. A strong scent of petrol. An aroma that always used to lift her heart, making her think of journeys and new beginnings.

Already, the cross in the sky had begun to dissolve. And as she watched, the truth hit like a bolt from the blue.

The cross wasn't lucky. It was a great big 'wrong' marked in the sky.

And it was meant for her.

Because she had been wrong – as wrong as anyone ever could be. And Gilbert was just like her. He was going to ruin his life too if someone didn't stop him.

Marie heard the airless *zip* without knowing what it was. There was a crackle like dry autumn leaves. A soft *boom*, close behind. Then heat, so sudden and fierce it felt as if the sun had fallen to earth.

She turned round, amazed. A wall of fire had sprung up. It encircled the whole of the East India Tyre Factory. The pile of tyres she had been sitting on only moments before burst into flames. Thick, black smoke began to pour as they melted into a mass of oozing rubber eels.

If I hadn't stood up to look at the cross, thought Marie, I'd already be gone.

She stared at the fire. Gilbert's fire. Made by his hands. He couldn't have known she was here. His fires were never meant to hurt anyone. It was just something that he had to do because fire was part of his chemistry.

As it had once been hers. She remembered that reckless feeling. That need for a life of adventure, following the promise of elsewhere, had burned up her whole life. Why hadn't she been able to control it? Why had she not taken control, as friends had urged her to do, when she'd come back and Martin had behaved so unreasonably over Gilbert? Why had she let him stop her seeing her own son?

Her heart had been on fire the night she had left Gilbert and his father. She had never meant to lose her son, always meant to come back and get him. The other man, waiting in the car, had promised they would.

A city girl, she'd felt so shut in and stifled in the small semi in the seaside town they had come to live in because housing was cheaper there. She'd met Martin in a city jazz club and, watching him play saxophone on a spot-lit stage, she thought she had found the key to the different, exotic life she craved.

At first she'd liked the fact that Martin was much older than she was because it made their relationship feel special and different. He seemed to know so much about the world.

Later, she realized he'd only read about it in books.

Too late, when she was stuck at home with a young baby while Martin worked as a car mechanic all day and went out, most nights, to play jazz in the seaside hotels – they needed the extra money, he said – only then did she realize that the elsewhere she had longed for was still somewhere else. She felt dead in her own life. It was a mundane nothingness, not what she'd wanted at all. She couldn't bear it.

And the promise of elsewhere was, in the end, what made her choose the other man; a man she used to work with in the city. She met him in the supermarket one Saturday morning when Gilbert was home with Martin. They had gone for a coffee.

And she ended up running away with him one damp autumn night.

Petrol fumes bunched round his car as he'd revved and revved, waiting for her. As they drove off she'd cried, clutching her arm where little Gilbert had clung to her, still feeling the weight of his head on her chest and the tickle of his eyelashes on her cheek. But the excitement of escape had been as strong as her guilt. She told herself she'd be right back for Gilbert, just as soon as she had sorted out her new life.

When they hit the motorway, the sight of the lights gave her a burst of the glittery feeling that she had lost in her life with Martin. She dried the tear-streaked make-up from her face and set a smile on her face. Back then, she'd been pretty. She had shiny dark hair and clear, bright skin. She wore make-up and perfume and nice clothes, in that other life that now seemed like a dream.

Not long after she'd left, she knew she'd done the wrong thing. The new man, Simon, wanted fun and excitement, but Marie found she couldn't live that life while aching for her abandoned child. And then she found out that Simon had been lying. He didn't want Gilbert with them after all.

He'd thought she would forget about him in her new life. Marie had been amazed. Forget her child?

She took the bus home. But Martin had reeled right back against the wall when he opened the door and saw her standing there, all red-eyed and dishevelled, eaten up with guilt. He'd pushed the door hard shut, wouldn't have anything to do with her, wouldn't let her in. She tried again and again, shouting through the letter box, pleading with him, telling him how stupid she had been to leave them like that.

But he wouldn't let her see Gilbert. He shouted from the other side of the door that she didn't have a son any more – she had lost the right to have him and she wasn't going to hurt him ever again.

That was when she began to feel like a shell-woman: empty, fragile and ready to break. Friends helped her find work, gave her a spare room to live in, even took her to a doctor who said that she needed a break from herself and put her on Prozac.

Get a lawyer and fight, said her friends. Martin has no right to keep you from your own son. But her friends didn't understand that she had no fight left. The pills nestled her in a cotton wool haze. The only way to find the will to fight was to cut the Prozac and climb out of the haze.

She couldn't do that. She needed sanctuary from the mess she'd made of her life.

And she began to doubt if Gilbert would want to see her. He must hate her for leaving him. How could she fight for a child who didn't love her?

But she could still love him. She could watch over him. And she did.

Through the railings of his school playground, from the end of a street, through the garden hedge of her old home, wherever she could. All her watching got in the way of normal life. She lost her job and gave up her friends. But she wouldn't give up on Gilbert, no matter how often Martin warned her off.

One day, she watched Martin load up a van and drive off with Gilbert. It took her long, panic-stricken weeks to track them, piecing together snippets of information she gathered from neighbours, to the caravan on the edges of Hungry. The relief when she found them again! She made up her mind to be ultra-careful, to make sure she was never seen, because then Martin might move on again and this time she might lose track of them forever.

Since then, she had watched over Gilbert every day of his life. She was part of the fabric of his life, though he never knew she was there.

She was his guardian angel. She watched out and worried over him, just like a mother. And being his guardian angel had brought her a kind of happiness.

But a guardian angel knew far more than an ordinary mother ever could. She knew more things about Gilbert than his father did. She'd seen how he was on the edges at school, left out because he didn't live in a nice house, didn't have the right clothes, wasn't quite like the others. As he'd grown up she'd seen his flashes of frustration at Martin and recognized the same mismatch of character between father and son as there had been between herself and Martin, because Gilbert was like her. All this summer, she'd watched the childhood fascination he'd had for matches and making harmless little bonfires outside the caravan, grow into something else. Something much bigger that he couldn't control.

What was the point of all her watching, all her guardian

angelship, if she couldn't do something to help her son when he needed her most?

The cross in the sky began to sag. The evening stood still. The fire blazed high and strong.

The fire was the work of Gilbert's hands. He had made it; it was his. Fire was his adventure, his sanctuary, his promise of elsewhere. But it was going to burn up his life.

There was one thing she could do. Something that would stop him.

Marie passed her tongue over dry lips. She thought of her special poem and knew why it cut to the heart of her. It told the story of her life. The poem had even foretold this moment, and the cross in the sky marked the spot where it would happen.

Burn me when I die, said the poem. *As I burned life.*

She would take all her courage and do the one thing she could that would rescue her son's life.

It won't be the first time I've been made of gilded splinters.

She took a step towards the fire. Then another.

If you cry when you remember me, thought Marie, as she walked into the fire of all fires, *Cry flames.*

Sapphire screamed.

A figure had walked right up to the wall of flame and set itself alight.

Gil was already out of the trees and running across the wasteland, making a dust storm of the dry ground. Sapphire followed, the shock and the dust in her eyes making her slow.

It seemed to take him ages to reach the burning figure, though it was only minutes – long enough for the person to be consumed by the fire. Sapphire could hardly watch as Gil punched a hand into the flames and pulled the burning figure to the ground. Now he was using his foot to roll it over and over, using the earth to quench the flames.

Sapphire looked around, desperate. No water anywhere. Only a scrap of tarpaulin. She used it to beat the last of the flames from the burnt body.

Then her legs gave way and she sat in the dust.

Gil stood over the body. He was shaking all over. One hand was red and scorched.

Sapphire could hardly look.

'It was deliberate,' she said, through chattering teeth. 'I saw.'

Gil said nothing. He sank to his knees beside the body.

'What'll we do?' whispered Sapphire. 'We need help.'

Gil put a shaking hand to the mouth of the burned face, feeling for a breath. The hands were too burned to search for a pulse. Suddenly, he drew back, and sat on his heels.

He turned to Sapphire. 'I think it's the woman at the bus stop. I think she's my mother.'

Sapphire stared at him, at the body on the ground.

'Your . . . ?'

It was hard to look at the face, but Sapphire did and even in its terrible state she recognized the fragile features.

The woman at the bus stop, the Mad Hatter, the cleaner from the Home was Gil's mother?

'I don't understand.'

Gil bent forward again until his head was close over the woman. Making a circle with the thumb and forefinger of his good hand, he placed it over the woman's mouth. He put his lips upon the circle, to avoid his lips touching the burnt face. Then he began to breathe into his mother's mouth.

He was giving her the kiss of life.

Sapphire's throat tightened. She bit her lip.

Behind them, the fire raged. Booms and crashes filled the air as the East India Tyre Factory imploded. From the direction of Hungry came the drone of a helicopter. The fire crews would be here in minutes.

Sapphire couldn't think of what would happen once she and Gil were found here, with the burnt woman beside the blazing wreck of the factory. If the fire crews and police found them here, everyone would decide she was unfit to be a mother. Probably she was. But they – the adult world – would take it upon themselves to determine what was to be done about her pregnancy. She and her body would have to do whatever was decided for her. Mum and Dad might not even have a say – now it might all be taken out of their hands and decided by social workers or a court.

And what would happen to Gil? They would find out he had been the firebug all along, and then what?

Gil stood up. He winced from the pain of his burnt hand.

'She's not breathing,' he said. 'I need to get Dad.'

Sapphire nodded. She gripped her hands together, sick and scared, wanting to get up and go with him.

'I'll wait here,' she said. 'She shouldn't be left alone.'

But the noise of the fire had brought Martin out of the caravan. He was already there.

Martin tried to find a breath or a pulsebeat in the body on the ground, but there was none. He looked up in horror.

'No, son, no. What are you saying? This isn't your mother.'

Gil hung his head. 'She is. I think she is.'

'No, Gilbert, no. What happened here? This wasn't you.'

Martin stared at his son, willing him to deny he had anything to do with this.

'She walked right into the fire,' said Gil. 'I tried to save her. It's the woman at the bus stop. The same one that used to hang around the school playground when I was little. I'm telling you, it's her.'

'Not your mother. No.'

Martin saw his son's scorched and shaking hand. He ripped a long strand of the bundle of sopping wet sheet he'd brought with him and bound up the hand.

'But *you* didn't make the fire. Why did you say that? It's never been you that's been doing all these fires.' Martin tucked in the end of the bandage. 'I don't believe it.'

'It's me,' said Gil. 'You know it's me. And you know it's her.'

Martin turned away and screwed up his eyes, avoiding his son's face, avoiding the face of the woman on the ground.

'I didn't kill her, Dad. I made the fire but she walked into it,' said Gil.

'She did,' said Sapphire. 'I saw her. She set herself on fire.'

Martin rubbed his forehead with his hand as if trying to scrub the image from his mind. He looked at Sapphire blankly.

The fire roared behind them. Its smoke stung their eyes, catching their throats.

Martin groaned softly. He shook out the wet sheet and bent to drop it gently over the woman's burnt face.

'She's a cleaner at the Home. She lives there,' said Sapphire. 'But there was something so strange about her – she'd stand at the bus stop for hours after work each night. I never saw her go anywhere, she'd just wait.'

The sound of sirens came from the far side of Hungry.

Martin stood staring at nothing.

'I'll tell them it's me,' said Gil at last.

'No,' said Sapphire. She turned to Gil's father. 'He's finished with that now. Aren't you, Gil? You couldn't do more fires, not now. Anyway, I lit it. It was me too.'

Martin blinked. He looked towards the road. The noise of sirens was growing by the second. The fire engines would be here any minute, and the police.

'They have to know what happened,' he said. His hands clenched and unclenched. 'Or it'll be a murder inquiry.'

'I'll tell them what I saw,' said Sapphire.

Gil shook his head. He touched her arm gently.

Martin looked bewildered. The girl was a stranger to him. He had no idea Gilbert had a girl.

'You two go to the caravan. I'll speak to them. I'll tell them what happened. That I saw her, that she did it herself. Though they'll want to know about the fires, Gil, and I don't know if I can sort it all, I . . .'

'It's all right, Dad.'

Gil looked and sounded as if he didn't care about what would happen to him. Sapphire could see he didn't want to leave his father alone.

'Go!' Martin pushed him towards the caravan. 'Take him,' he told Sapphire. 'I'll talk to the police. But Gilbert – the fires must stop. Never again, Gilbert. Never.'

Gil looked at the burned-up figure on the ground that was his mother. He clenched and unclenched his fists just as Martin had done.

'Never,' he said. 'It's the end.'

Though Gil knew, and his father didn't say, that they were not at the end of this at all.

*

Martin watched them run. As they reached the caravan, the fire engines sped on to the wasteland in clouds of dust. Martin just had time to bend over the woman to take a closer look at the scorched and rusted silver locket that had caught his eye. It hung like a tarnished moon at the dead woman's neck, hanging just below the sheet that he had placed over her face.

Martin stared. The smell of the woman's burnt flesh made him flinch. He checked her hand and there was the ring he'd once given her. She'd never taken it off. He clenched his teeth and gently prised open the locket with a thumbnail.

Inside, was a tiny tooth. A child's tooth. As small and perfect as a frozen teardrop.

Martin snapped the clasp shut. Trembling, he placed the locket close to the woman's heart, bowed his head and knelt beside the body, with the heat and fury of the blaze on his back, and a great chill in his heart.

They didn't do what Martin said. They didn't go into the caravan but slipped behind it to the fairy ring of birch trees until the fire squads and police were gathered on the wasteland. They stayed there in the bramble bushes and long grass, out of sight of the circling helicopter. Finally, when it was dark enough, they ran down the open stretch of the Great Western Road – ran for the cover of the tree-lined streets of Hungry, and kept running until they reached their haven in the grounds of Hunger Home.

In the time it took them to get there, a thousand stars punctured the sky. They lay in the trees, not talking, thoughts spinning as uselessly as the helicopter that circled Hungry's streets.

'Let's walk,' said Sapphire, when the helicopter had given up.

In the darkness, Gil saw only broken things – cracked pavements, a flickering streetlight, smashed bottles, a torn fence, crooked railings and the shatter of stars. The world felt very fragile.

Neither of them looked in the direction of the East India Tyre Factory, but the smell of burnt rubber seeped into the streets.

Deep in the night, they passed a sprinkler illicitly drenching a garden lawn. Sapphire unwrapped the bandage on Gil's scorched hand, stood under the sprinkler to wet and clean it, then wrapped it back around his burns. She broke their silence.

'You really know it was her? You're sure?'

'His face told me.'

Sapphire nodded. She'd seen the look on his father's face too.

'But you didn't kill her, Gil. She did it.'

'It was my fire.'

'Ours,' Sapphire corrected him. 'It was our fire.'

'Ours then.' Gil paused. 'She must have hated her life to want to finish it like that. Did she think I hated her? Why did she do it?'

Sapphire couldn't answer, she could only hold his uninjured hand.

'I'll never forget,' said Gil.

'I know,' said Sapphire.

But maybe we won't always feel like this, she thought, remembering what Mrs Merry had said that day in the reading room. Most people get over most things, she'd said. It all fades. In ten years, wondered Sapphire, what will we feel about all this? It won't be like tonight.

'We won't forget,' she said.

She heard the echo of the Moreau in her mum's photo den.

It doesn't last . . . it fades . . . and after it is gone . . .

'But it'll fade,' she told Gil and she hoped that was true.

Sapphire stopped on the grass verge. They'd walked right through Hungry and had reached the crossroads where the long straight road that went right into the heart of the city was intersected by the curve of the one which led, whether you turned right or left, into the circular street maze of Hungry.

The darkness was beginning to lift. There had only been a few hours of night, hardly enough for the air to cool before the sun rose to restoke the heat.

The curving road would take Sapphire home; the straight road to the city. If she took the Hungry road, she'd have the baby. Then give it away and lose her peace of mind or keep it and lose herself.

Sapphire thought of the other road. The one that led to the place where she could end the tiny scrap of life inside her – and salvage her own.

A lorry slowed down and its young driver stared out of the window. He ignored Gil but gestured to Sapphire that she could have a lift. She looked at her feet and shook her head. Gil took a step forward and the lorry rumbled off.

'I'll walk you home,' said Gil, staring after the lorry. Its radio was playing the song he'd been hearing all summer long. 'It's safer.'

Sapphire gave a soft laugh. 'When did you bother about being safe?'

Life is risking. Had she told him that? But he didn't need Jeanne Moreau or anyone else to tell him that. Gil knew.

Sapphire looked ahead to the city. She looked over her

shoulder at Hungry Hill. Everyone'll hate me, whatever I do. So I may as well do what I want.

Over in the direction of the fairy ring a haze of smoke, made luminous by the dawn, drifted. Burnt rubber still tainted the air.

I wish it would rain, thought Sapphire. She turned to Gil. There had been so many better moments. This wasn't the right one at all, but it was the only one left. Sapphire moved close and kissed him. He didn't expect it and flinched, as if she'd hurt him.

The kiss flashed all through her, across her skin, rushing along her veins, into every part of her, until it hit the back wall of her heart. And it rushed through Gil too; she felt the heat burn through his clothes.

Sapphire pulled back. Gil felt dazed. He touched his mouth with his scorched hand. He forgot the pain, so amazed was he that she'd kissed him. He didn't know what to do or say.

Sapphire sat down on the grass verge and put her face in her hands. 'I'm in a mess, Gil,' she blurted. 'A great big one. As big as yours. I have to decide what to do and I don't know. It's killing me.'

He sat down beside her.

'You can tell me,' he offered.

'I already have,' she said through her fingers, 'but you never heard.'

'Tell me again and this time I'll hear.'

She shook her head. There were already too many people involved. She had to deal with this on her own. And it would change things between them if he knew. He'd see her differently. It had happened each time – with her parents, with Miranda and even Emma. She wouldn't risk it with Gil.

Gil sat down beside her and asked no more. He thought about what he would face when he went back home.

'When you come to a fork in the road, take it,' he said after a while.

Sapphire took her face out of her hands and looked out at the intersecting roads.

'Guess who said that?' said Gil.

Sapphire shrugged.

'Give up?' said Gil.

'Haven't a clue.'

He grinned. 'Yogi Bear.'

Sapphire found herself smiling back. It was too silly.

'The cartoon?'

'Uhuh. Yogi, the smartest bear that ever lived.'

Sapphire gave a wobbly laugh. 'But what does that mean? Which one do you take?'

'That's the point.' Gil shook his head and slipped his good hand in hers. 'You *have* to take the fork, one way or another, or you just stand in one place, stuck, and that's worse. See? When you come to a fork in the road, just take it.'

Sapphire laughed. 'I get it.'

Yogi was right. She couldn't stay stuck forever. She had to choose, and soon, or someone would make the choice for her.

Most people, Mrs Merry said, get over most things. The old woman had, and so had two out of three women in the magazine article. All those people had coped with the inescapable fact that the rescue of their own life meant the end of a tiny one that had hardly begun.

Whatever she did, there would be a price to pay.

And Gil had his own price to pay. A boy with a burnt hand, living next to a petrol station, right next to the fire of all fires – he had the police to face; he surely would. And beyond all that, he'd have to live with the knowledge that he'd played a part in the death of his own mother.

There were things they had to live through, and they would.

The road home wound in tight, decreasing circles until it stopped at the far side of Hungry Hill, in the dead end where the buses about-turned to go back into the city. The Great Western Road stretched ahead, the only way out of Hungry. It led all the way to the city – and the clinic.

Sapphire turned to Gil, pulled his face close to hers, and kissed him again. The kiss told her something about herself that she needed right now. She was as scared as she would ever be – but the kiss shot through all that, filling her with such a sensation of her own self that she knew, with the certainty of a compass, which direction she would take.

It was a very straight road. Sapphire put one hand on her heart, the other on her stomach, and sent a bolt of utter sorrow from the depths of herself to the tiny stranger inside. She couldn't send love because she didn't feel that.

'I've got to go,' she told Gil. 'So have you. But we'll be OK in the end.'

He wondered about that because without fire he was just Gilbert Lemon. A shadow who lived at the back of beyond; who had to go back there and face up to his mother's death, and his part in that.

Yet now he was real. Sapphire had made him real. She had given him a kiss of life. And his mother – with a shock he saw that she had done the same.

The shadow Gilbert Lemon had lived in died on the spot and all of a sudden he was right there in his body. Strong and real. He felt it happen.

He thought of the song that had been running through his head all summer, about the girl who left everything to live on the moon and travel the stars. The girl with Jupiter drops in her hair.

He thought of the woman who had crashed back to earth, back into his life, when he never thought she would. But the journey back had burned her up. That's the way he would think of her – as an amazing thing like a shooting star, hurtling out of the night into a final radiance. She had walked right into his fire, so she must have done it for him.

'I'll come back soon,' said Sapphire. 'I promise.'

She linked her little finger with the little finger of his good hand, and he believed her.

Then she stood up, looking so scared that Gil got up too and tried to keep hold of her.

But she pulled away and stepped out on to the Great Western Road.

Gil let her go.

Each time Sapphire looked back, he was still at the crossroads. And something in the way he stood watching her, for as long as she could still see him, said he'd wait there a while, still burning from her kiss.